FRIENDS
OF ACPL

THE KING WHO RIDES A TIGER

❀❀❀ and Other Folk Tales from Nepal

THE KING
WHO RIDES A TIGER

and Other Folk Tales from Nepal

✿✿✿✿✿✿✿✿ by Patricia Hitchcock

with illustrations by Lillian Sader ✿✿✿✿

PARNASSUS PRESS BERKELEY, CALIFORNIA

1386111

❀❀❀ TO ALL THE *Madhu Thapas, Emilys, Shri Rams, Marions, Prem Bahadurs, and Little Bens who love to sit by the fire and hear fairy tales, these stories are lovingly dedicated.*

❀❀❀ Contents

Introduction

❀❀❀ Nepal, land of Mount Everest, the earth's highest peak, and home of the sturdy Sherpas, is an independent kingdom on the southwest slope of the Himalayan Range, between India and Tibet. Isolated by steep mountains and rugged terrain, few strangers visit this remote land where hearty farmers and shepherds, with their families, follow nature and the seasons in their daily life and work.

When spring comes to the Himalayas of western Nepal the hill shepherds prepare themselves for the long, unbroken season of hard work and separation that faces them. The fields around their winter homes in the valley are first plowed and planted to corn. A year's supply of wood is cut from the jungle and hauled into each courtyard. One or two members of the family may be sent several miles above the village to plant potatoes in the alpine meadows still encircled with melting snow. Then, when the grass begins to appear on the steep slopes above the meadows, the shepherds strip down their cattle sheds, pack their kitchen needs into baskets, and travel with this equipment to these high mountain pastures, herding their animals up the trails ahead of them. Someone, usually a grandmother, stays home to look after the corn. Another person, often an older girl, is spared from herding long enough to return home for food whenever the shepherds need it. She takes her grandmother potatoes when they are big enough to eat, and returns to her father with news of the village and the ripening crop.

In September the shepherds feel it is time to leave. They herd their animals back down the trails to their valley homes, carrying their sheds, kettles, and potatoes with them. Then the family is once more united. Before the snow falls, the corn is harvested and barley is planted on the bare fields. There is little to do then, but wait out the weeks of cold weather that lie ahead.

This is the time when women and children are seen scurrying along the terrace paths to the house of a favorite storyteller. The little room is lit only by the light of the hearth fire. It is crowded with aunts, cousins, sisters—all huddled together. Hands are busy spinning. But spinning is no chore when there are jokes and stories to tell. Someone blows on the fire to send the smoke away. Faces brighten. Then the laughter suddenly stops. The tale has begun: "Once, during the reign of a great king . . ."

Here are some of the tales you would hear in the Valley of the Bhuji River if you were the daughter of Chiga Magarni or the son of Tek Bahadur Poon.

Soonimaya ❀❀❀

❀❀❀❀❀❀❀ Once, during the reign of a great king, there lived a little girl named Soonimaya, the daughter of a hill shepherd, Mahn Singh, and his wife, Dahn Jita. The three had a very happy life together. In the summertime they wandered with their flocks over the high mountain pastures of Dhor, and in the wintertime before the snows came to close the pass, they came down to their stone house in the river valley of Neeshee to plant corn.

When Soonimaya was ten years old her mother, Dahn Jita, fell sick and died. For days Soonimaya grieved. Mahn Singh did not know what to do to comfort her. Finally he decided to marry a widow whose husband had left her with a girl Soonimaya's age and a boy a few years younger. "In this way," thought Mahn Singh, "my little girl will have a sister and a mother, and I will have a wife and a son."

After they had lived together for a while, Mahn Singh knew he would have a difficult time caring for such a large family. His little flock of goats and sheep was too small.

There was no money for clothes or peppers. One day he told his wife: "I will go into the army so I can send money home every year. Then, when you have bought enough animals and land to feed us all, I will come home to stay."

Now the stepmother treated Soonimaya as well as she did her own children while Mahn Singh was at home, but as soon as he left for the army she began to treat Soonimaya differently. She made her stay up all night to guard the flock after working all day in the fields. She gave her husks to eat instead of the good rice she cooked for her own children. But Soonimaya never complained.

One day the stepmother sent Soonimaya into the jungle to bring fodder for the animals, but she would not give her a kukari, a large hunting knife, to cut the leaves or a tumpline to carry them home. Soonimaya went into the jungle and wept. When some snakes came by and asked her why she was crying, she told them what the stepmother expected of her.

"Stop crying, Soonimaya," said the snakes. "We will crawl up into the trees and cut some branches for you, if you will gather the leaves. Then, when we have a good load, you can make us into a tumpline and we will help you carry the fodder home. Set us down gently, so we won't get hurt, and we will slip back into the forest."

Soonimaya gathered the leaves as fast as the snakes threw them down from the trees, and she piled them into a big bundle.

When the stepmother saw the load of fodder Soonimaya had brought home, she was very puzzled. "I will have to think of something she cannot do at all," she thought to herself. "Then I can send her away for disobeying me, and her father will not blame me when he returns."

Some time later the stepmother gave Soonimaya a sieve

and told her to bring some water from the spring. Soonimaya knew this would be a hopeless task, but she went to
the spring with the sieve as she was told. She tried and tried
to make the sieve hold water. She cupped her hands under
it, she lined it with leaves, she filled the holes with clay. But
always, before she reached home, the sieve would be
empty. Finally she sat down on a stone near the spring and
wept.

Some ants came out of the ground and asked Soonimaya
why she was weeping.

"My stepmother expects me to carry water in this," she
moaned, holding up the sieve so they could see it. "What
shall I do?"

"Stop crying," pleaded the ants when they heard her
story. "We will help you. Each of us will sit over a hole in
the sieve and you can fill it with water. When you get home
pour the water very slowly into your storage jar. Then tap
the sieve lightly with a stick and we will fall to the ground
and come back to the spring."

Soonimaya was grateful to the ants and did just as she
was told. When the stepmother saw the water in the storage jar, she was surprised and annoyed. "This girl is too
clever," thought the wicked woman. "I shall have to find a
more dangerous task."

When the monsoon arrived the stepmother told Soonimaya to go into the jungle to get some tiger's milk for her
stepbrother and sister. Soonimaya did not know how she
could obey without being eaten by the tiger. She started into
the jungle with her wooden pot, but the trail was so slippery
she fell after every few steps. Finally she sat down on a big
rock and wept from fear and exhaustion.

Now it happened that under the rock lived a mother
tigress and her four baby kittens. The kittens heard Sooni-

maya crying and came out to see what was the matter.
When Soonimaya told them the task her stepmother had
set for her, they said:

"Do not cry so loudly, Soonimaya, or our mother will
wake up and eat you! Give us your taykee and we will fill it
while she is asleep."

Soonimaya sat very still while the tiger kittens disappeared into the den to collect the milk. When they returned
she hugged them all and hurried home to give the milk to
her brother and sister. The stepmother saw her children
drinking the tiger's milk and stared. "This girl is a witch,"
she muttered to herself. "I must get rid of her."

It was a long time before she thought of something else
for Soonimaya to do. Finally she said to her, "I need a
Champa flower for some medicine. Get me one."

Soonimaya walked to the base of the mountain that rose
up steeply behind her village and looked for a way to climb
to the high shelf where the Champa flowers grew. There
was no path and she could not find footholds in the cliff.
After a few hours she gave up in despair. A big vulture,
seeing her distress, swept down and landed on the ground
in front of her.

"Oh, Little Sister, why are you so upset?" he asked,
hopping nearer.

Soonimaya told him as well as she could between sobs.

"Well now, this is a problem we can solve," said the
vulture cheerfully. "Hang on tight and I will carry you up."

Before the tears had dried on her cheeks, Soonimaya
found herself aloft on the back of the big bird, sailing up
and up, above the valley floor to the top of the mountain.
Suddenly her ride came to an end and she was tossed, with
a swoosh and a bump, into a bed of beautiful Champa

flowers. The bird and the girl laughed with pleasure.

While they sat looking out over the valley, the vulture spied a number of his relatives circling the river to the south.

"Something is going on down there," he said to Sooni-maya. "I will have to leave you for a little while, but pick all the flowers you want and I will come back to carry you home."

The vulture swung into the air and soared out across the valley toward the river. Soonimaya watched the flight of her friend, then turned her eyes to the main road winding along far below her. She saw travelers moving up and down the narrow trail. Some of them were carrying heavy loads and some were walking behind herds of goats. Tiny bells tinkled in the wind. One of the travelers was a soldier coming up the trail with two porters, each laboring under the weight of a trunk. She watched the lowry as he sat down under a tree to rest. Suddenly she recognized him! He was her own father coming home on leave, with wonderful presents for everyone.

"Oh, Ba! Ba!" she shouted, jumping and waving her arms to catch his attention. But Soonimaya, forgetting where she was in her excitement, slipped and fell to her death.

Word of Mahn Singh's homecoming had already reached the village. People ran to tell him the terrible news and to take him to the foot of the cliff. When Mahn Singh reached his little girl he was overcome with sorrow. He carried her to a place near the river and buried her there. Slowly his sorrow changed to anger. "What was Soonimaya doing on such a high cliff?" he said to himself. He went straight home to his wife and demanded an answer.

"I don't know," said the deceitful woman, "I told her not to go up there, but she would not obey me. Oh dear!" she sighed, "I expected something like this would happen, because she did very strange things. She was never quite the same after you left, you know. Why, she even tried to carry water in a sieve!"

When the evil stepmother thought she had calmed her husband, she cooked him a fine meal of curried chicken and long, white rice. She gave him wine of three-waters and rubbed his tired legs. But Mahn Singh, though his anger slowly left him, still felt deeply the loss of his little daughter. He stayed only a week at home before he returned to the army.

A few days later, a beautiful golden pillar sprang up from the ground where Mahn Singh had buried Soonimaya. A blacksmith passing by saw it and hurried to report it to the king.

"Bring it at once!" was the order. "So I may judge its worth."

The king stood in awe of the golden pillar. Never had anything like it been brought to the palace. He reached out to feel the gold with his hands, and instantly the pillar turned into a beautiful young girl.

The king was delighted.

"See what has come to us!" he exclaimed to his courtiers. "Is this not a fitting bride for my eldest son?"

All the people of the palace were enchanted with the girl who had sprung from the golden pillar. They knew the king had been searching everywhere for a bride for their favorite prince, and at last one had been found. Now, amidst great rejoicing, the wedding preparations began.

News of the marriage went out all over the country and soon it reached the ears of Mahn Singh's wicked wife. She was very disappointed, for she had hoped her own daughter would one day be the queen.

Months later the king announced the birth of a son to the happily married pair. Everyone in the country was invited to the naming feast. The wicked stepmother was so eager to see the princess that she was the first to arrive at the palace on the feast day. She turned pale with astonishment to find that the girl sitting beside the handsome prince, holding the baby in her arms, was Soonimaya.

When the stepmother returned home, she said to her daughter: "You will never guess who is the mother of the baby prince. Soonimaya!" Squatting by the fire, she added: "And to think someday she will be queen over us all."

After a long pause, she coughed and said: "You look enough like your stepsister to be her twin. Why not go to the palace tomorrow to visit her? After you are acquainted again, you can invite her to the river for a swim. Perhaps she might have an accident and drown. Remember, the girl who is married to the eldest prince will someday be the queen."

The daughter, who had grown as wicked as her mother, would have done anything to become the queen. She carefully packed a basket full of food and presents, and set out the next morning for the palace. When she was shown into the room where the princess was sitting, she rushed over and, covering her head with her shawl, bowed very low in a gesture of great respect. Soonimaya returned the greeting graciously and ordered tea brought for both of them.

"Sister," said the visitor, after she had given Soonimaya the presents and talked a while. "The day is full of sunshine. Let us go to the river and bathe together."

Soonimaya could think of no good reason to stay at

home, so she strapped her little son onto her back and left the palace with her stepsister. When they reached the river, the stepsister said:

"The water is much clearer over here in this lovely big pool. I will hold Baby Lakshman for you while you take your swim, and you can hold him while I take mine."

Soonimaya did not notice that the pool was very deep. She handed Lakshman to her companion, removed her velvet blouse and golden sari, and turned to step into the river. At that moment the stepsister pushed Soonimaya. The princess lost her balance, tumbled into the pool, and sank out of sight. The girl on the bank dressed quickly in Soonimaya's beautiful clothes, strapped the baby onto her back, and hurried up the trail to the palace.

Everyone, including the prince, thought the girl who returned from the river was Soonimaya. Only Baby Lakshman knew she was not his mother; when it was time for him to nurse he began to fret, and soon he was crying loudly.

When Soonimaya sank down into the deep pool she came to the home of two large water snakes. She bowed to each in turn, very politely. The male snake was so surprised he said:

"When we saw you coming we were planning to eat you, but since you have greeted us with such respect we will spare your life for three days."

That night Soonimaya asked the snakes if she could go back to the palace to nurse her little son. The snakes consented to let her go if she promised to return to the river before dawn. Soonimaya readily agreed and left for the palace. She circled the courtyard to avoid being seen in the moonlight, ran up the long flight of stairs to the balcony, and stole cautiously along the wall to the nursery door. In

her haste she failed to notice a tailor, wrapped in a blanket,
lying against the balcony wall. He had not been able to go
to sleep because of the baby's crying. The tailor was startled
to see a woman walk past him in the middle of the night,
but he lay very still. Soonimaya unbolted the door and
slipped inside. At once the baby stopped crying. "That is an
unusual way for the princess to enter the palace," the tailor
thought to himself. "And why does she let the baby cry so
long before she feeds him?"

When the visitor left the nursery just before dawn, in the
same mysterious fashion, the tailor was even more puzzled.

The tailor worked hard all the next day, but by sundown
he still had not finished his master's vest. He set his work
aside, lay down, and rolled up in his blanket. He was awakened from sleep by the cries of Baby Lakshman, and soon
after, he heard the light step of feet on the stairway. He
opened his eyes and saw Soonimaya, again entering the
nursery.

Some time after the baby had been quieted, the princess
departed in the same stealthy manner. The tailor sat up and
peered through the carved grill of the balcony. He watched
his mistress circle the courtyard, run along the shadow
of the garden wall, and hurry down the trail to the river.
"Something very strange is going on," he thought. "When
the prince awakens, I will tell him all I have seen."

As soon as the prince heard the tailor's story he said, "We
will both watch tonight. If the woman comes again, we will
catch her and make her tell us what she is doing."

That night the prince hid in a corner of the balcony and
the tailor lay against the balcony wall under his blanket.
Baby Lakshman began to cry, as usual, because he was
now very hungry. About midnight the tailor saw the

woman running up the hill toward the palace. "Here she comes, Sahib-ji," he whispered to the prince. They both watched her circle the courtyard and run forward to the palace stairs. They heard her footsteps as she climbed to the balcony. In another moment she had reached the nursery door, lifted the latch, and gone inside. Instantly the baby stopped crying. The prince ran to the door and peeked into the room. There he saw Soonimaya holding little Lakshman in her arms, rocking him gently while he nursed. The prince knew at once that this was his son's real mother. When Lakshman had finished nursing, Soonimaya bathed him with warm, sweet oil and laid him in his cradle. Then, with tears in her eyes, she kissed him and turned to leave. But when she reached the door the prince jumped up and caught her.

"Oh, please!" she begged. "Do not detain me. The snakes in the river gave me three days' grace to live, and they permitted me to visit Lakshman if I promised to return before dawn. Perhaps if I keep my promise they will spare my life a little longer."

But the prince would not let her go. He took her inside the palace and made her tell him everything.

Now, it was the habit of the stepsister to rise very early in the morning to go for a walk. This morning she was up at the usual time and out walking in the garden. Just as the sun came up, the palace was aroused by a terrible scream! Everyone rushed out to see what was the matter and there, disappearing in the distance, were two large snakes, dragging a girl down the trail to the river.

"The princess!" shouted the excited cook. "Get your kukaris!"

"But there is the princess!" answered the shepherd boy,

pointing to the balcony.

Great was the rejoicing when everyone discovered the real Soonimaya was standing by her husband's side.

The stepmother was banished from the kingdom forever, and the prince and Soonimaya were able, at last, to live happily ever after with the little baby named Lakshman, who never had to go hungry again.

The Perfect Husband ❁❁❁

❁❁❁❁❁❁❁ About two days walk from the village of Gorkha, there lived in a den on the side of a mountain a very brave tiger, his wife, and three baby cubs. Nearby, in a drab hideaway, lived a very cowardly fox.

The fox noticed that all the animals of the forest admired the courage and daring of the tiger. "Why," he thought to himself, "should everyone admire him and not admire me? I will make them think I am just as brave as the tiger."

From that day on, the fox boasted of his exploits to anyone who would give him an audience, and many of his listeners began to believe him. The only one he failed to convince at all was the tigress.

"Oh, listen to him," said the tigress one day when she heard him bragging to a cluster of monkeys. "What nonsense! All my husband has to do is to look at him and he runs away."

The monkeys chattered and laughed but the fox was not pleased. "It is time," he said to himself, "to teach that haughty tigress a lesson."

The next morning he waited patiently behind a tree until he saw the father tiger leave to go hunting. Then he walked up to the den and shouted to the tigress.

"Oh, Elder Brother's Wife! Where is Elder Brother?"

"He has gone hunting," came the reply.

"Well, that's lucky for him," said the fox, "because if he had been here I would have kicked him for killing my chickens."

None of the animals of the forest ever dared talk about the tiger this way. The tigress was surprised but she said nothing. The fox finally went away.

The next morning, after the tiger had gone hunting, again the fox returned and called out to the tigress in the same manner.

"Oh, Elder Brother's Wife! Where is Elder Brother?"

"He has gone hunting," she answered.

"Well, he IS lucky," shouted the fox. "If he had been here I would have pushed him over the cliff for stealing my rabbits."

The tigress did not answer the fox, but when her husband came home that night she told him how the fox had come in the mornings and accused him of stealing his rabbits and killing his chickens.

"He said he would kick you or push you off the cliff."

"Let him come again tomorrow," said the tiger angrily. "Tell him I have gone hunting and we will see how brave he is."

The next morning, after the fox saw the tiger leave his den, he went up to the door and shouted to the tigress.

"Oh, Elder Brother's Wife! Where is Elder Brother?"

"You just missed him," answered the tigress. "He has already gone hunting."

"What a coward!" shouted the fox in a voice that could be heard all over the forest. "Doesn't he ever catch anything to eat that lasts for more than a day? Why, if I could see him now I would. . . .”

The tiger, listening nearby, had heard enough. He sprang out of his hiding place, roaring with anger. The fox was terrified! He fled through the trees, dashing this way and that, trying desperately to think of an idea that would save him from the jaws of the angry tiger. Suddenly he saw a hollow log beside the trail. He bolted into it, hoping the tiger would run by. But the tiger, seeing the end of the fox's tail disappearing into the log, rushed in after him.

The tiger was running so fast he did not notice that the log was only big enough to let a fox through at the other end. About halfway in, he could go no farther. The more he struggled to get out, the worse things became—until he finally could not move at all. There in the middle of the log he stuck, while the fox squeezed through to freedom.

The fox hovered about warily until he was sure the tiger would never come out again. Then he ran back to the tigress to tell her what had happened.

“You should have seen me!” he boasted, kicking his heels and snapping his teeth. “Your husband was so frightened that he flung himself into the river. I tried to save him but he drowned.”

The tigress, at first, did not even seem to be interested; she thought the fox was boasting as usual. But after many days had passed, and her husband did not return, she began to believe the fox's story. At last she said to her cubs:

“It is difficult for me to get food and to keep house at the same time. I will marry the brave fox so we will have a good hunter in the family.”

The fox, who had been waiting for just such an opportunity, was delighted. He married the tigress and they settled down to housekeeping in the tiger's den.

The following day the wife sent her new husband into

the jungle to find some food. But he was more interested in sleeping than hunting, so he found a lovely glade of oak trees and lay down for a long nap. When he awoke, at sunset, he was hungry. Quickly and quietly he stole into a farmer's courtyard and caught a big fat chicken, but instead of taking it home to share with the tigress and her cubs, he sat down in a safe place in the forest and ate it all up. When he arrived back at the den empty-handed, the tigress was very upset.

"What do you expect us to do?" she complained. "The children are hungry and there is nothing for them to eat!"

"I roamed over the whole jungle all day," whined the fox. "But nothing I found was good enough to feed my family. I wanted to bring home a surprise."

"I like surprises," retorted the tigress. "But I would have preferred something to eat. However," she added, pleased that her husband thought she and her cubs were worthy of something special, "tomorrow I will go with you and we will get something good for all of us."

The next morning the tigress left the cubs in the den and went out with her husband to get some food. The two had not been gone long, before they found some cattle grazing in a small valley that funneled into a narrow draw.

"You go up above them" whispered the tigress, "and chase them down the valley. I will hide at the foot of the draw and catch the fat bull as he comes by."

The fox climbed above the cattle as his wife suggested. Then he ran down upon them and tried to chase them through the draw. Most of the animals were frightened and fled. But the fat bull did not like being chased. He stood very still, pretending to eat, until the fox was almost upon him. Then he ducked his horns between his legs and quickly swung his head upwards. The blow caught the fox between the ribs and lifted him high into the air. He fell with a terrible thud and lay sprawled out on the ground as if he were dead. When he woke up he knew he had been lying in the hot sun for a long time.

"What on earth have you been doing?" asked the tigress when at last she saw him coming towards her. "Where is the big fat bull?"

"I hunted all over but I could not find the animal you described," replied the fox. "The sun was so hot I lay down for a minute, and I must have fallen asleep."

The tigress was in no mood for excuses, but she did not want to start an argument with her new husband so she obligingly offered a compromise.

"I will find the big fat bull," she suggested, "if you will stay here and catch him as he comes by."

The fox thought this would be easy and he was glad to agree. He lay down and waited in the cool shade of the cliff, whisking the flies away with his tail, while his wife went off to round up the cattle.

He had almost fallen asleep when he heard the cattle coming. The rumble of their hoofs echoed through the canyon and clouds of dust billowed up from the valley floor. This so frightened the fox he ran up onto a high ledge and let the bawling herd thunder past beneath him. When the dust settled he noticed an old bullock, that had been trampled to death by the others, lying in the bottom of the draw.

"What luck!" he said to himself. He picked up a big stick and ran down to stand beside the bullock, just as his wife came hurrying around the bend.

"This big fellow would not give up!" panted the fox, heaving his chest up and down as if the struggle had exhausted him.

The tigress looked once at the old bullock and began to complain. "But this is not the one I told you to get. This is just a tough old bullock. Why didn't you catch the tender young bull?"

"My dear," answered the fox in his most condescending manner, "it is obvious that you do not know meat the way I do. This animal you call a 'tough old bullock' is the best for eating. He is all meat. The fat young bull you wanted me to get would have been all fat. Fat without any meat tastes terrible!"

He made such a face the tigress thought that perhaps he knew what he was talking about.

"Well, at least he is big," she admitted. "Now comes the work of carrying him home."

"Are you telling me I have to carry this bullock?" inquired the fox. "Ha! I am a man. A man should not have to carry anything if he has a wife along, but I want to be helpful so I will offer to carry the lungs."

The tigress said nothing. With one sweep of her paws she pulled the lungs out of the carcass and handed them to her husband. Then, like a dutiful wife, she picked up the rest of the bullock, flung it over her shoulder, and started home.

As the two traveled together through the forest, they came to a deep ravine that had washed away the trail during the summer rains. Someone had felled a huge tree and had wrestled it into place to make a bridge. The tigress stepped up onto the trunk of the tree and walked along it with ease, skillfully balancing her heavy load. But the fox was afraid he would fall off. He scurried this way and that, trying to find enough courage to start across. When the tigress reached the other side, she dropped to the trail and turned around to see why the fox was not following.

"What's the matter?" she called back. "Are you afraid you will fall off?"

"Of course not," came the injured reply. "I just wanted to see if this would make a good pounding pole for hulling rice."

The tigress had not expected that for an answer. "Imagine having a husband who thinks about pounding poles for rice while he is out hunting," she mused as she walked ahead.

When the tigress had disappeared, the fox dashed down into the ravine and up the other side to join her.

A little farther along, they came to a large boulder that had fallen across the trail. The tigress skimmed over it easily and walked on. Suddenly she realized that her husband was not coming behind her. She turned around and saw him leaping and clawing at the top of the rock, his head bobbing into view with every jump.

"Are you having trouble?" she shouted. "Is it too high for you?"

"Don't be silly!" answered the indignant fox. "I am just testing this rock to see if it will make a good grindstone."

"My other husband never noticed these things," thought the happy tigress to herself as she turned again to the trail.

The fox waited to be sure she would not see him. Then he ran around the rock as fast as he could and dashed after her.

At a bend in the trail they came to a place where there had been a small landslide. There was no way to cross without jumping. This posed no problem for the tigress. She leaped across without any trouble. But the fox was afraid of falling into the river.

"Aren't you coming?" called the tigress when she failed to hear her husband's footsteps behind her. But this time there was no answer. When the tigress turned around, the fox was nowhere in sight. She ran back to the landslide and there he was, far below, swinging in a vine.

"Oh dear! You fell!" she exclaimed.

"No, I did not fall," the fox assured her. "I wanted to see if this would make a good rope to tie our buffalo."

The tigress grinned down at him, unable to conceal her pleasure. She had never known a man to be so interested in pounding poles and grindstones and ropes, before he actually needed them.

"Shall I help you climb up?" she asked with an air of affection.

"Oh, no. That won't be necessary," answered the fox. He must not appear to need his wife's assistance. "You run along and I will catch up with you when I get this vine measured properly."

As soon as the tigress had gone beyond hearing distance, the fox began his struggle to get back to the trail. He pulled and tugged and scratched his way upward, tearing the lungs to shreds on the thorns that stood in his way.

When he finally caught up with the tigress, she noticed he had only a little piece of the lungs left.

"What happened to the rest of the lungs?" she asked, looking at him suspiciously.

"Well, my dear," began the fox, "I met many of my friends along the way. I had to give them something as a token of my respect, so I gave each one a piece of the lungs."

"You don't have that many friends!" jeered the tigress.

"How do you know how many friends I have?" retorted the fox. "I have many more than you do."

"Well, you don't!" said the tigress emphatically.

"All right, if you have so many friends, call them,"

challenged the fox. "Let me see how many there are."

The tigress, now offended, dropped the old bullock on the ground. She would show the fox how many friends she had. She threw back her head and started to roar. Soon she was roaring so loudly that she could be heard in every village in the valley. And the more she roared the more she frightened everyone, until at last the only answer to her roars was the whisper of the wind in the high branches.

When the tigress was hoarse from roaring, the fox said: "Now I will show you how many friends I have." He sauntered out to a point overlooking the valley and began to bark. As soon as the other foxes in the jungle heard him, they began to bark too. The jackals and the village dogs began to bark. Soon the whole valley seemed to be filled with barking animals.

The tigress was amazed. She couldn't believe it. But what more did she need to convince her that the fox had friends in every village in the district of Gorkha? She looked at her husband with new respect. Had he not been very brave in his fight with the tiger? Was he not clever at picking out good meat? And did he not always try to find better tools to make housekeeping easier? Now he had also shown her he was famous. She picked up the old bullock and headed once more toward home. "In fact," she muttered to herself as she trotted along, "for a husband he is just about perfect."

When the fox and his wife arrived at the den, the three little cubs greeted them eagerly, and they all sat down for a long feast on the old bullock.

Walking two days distance from the village of Gorkha, any traveler will find, even today, the little family living happily together. If the traveler stops briefly, he will observe the fox still trying to prove himself the perfect husband for a tigress.

How
the Travelers Shared Their Meal

❀❀❀❀❀❀❀ Three men, all traveling from different
villages to the spring festival in Pearsing, met for the first
time at a large resting place under a shady peepul tree.

The three travelers looked very different sitting together
on the big chowtara under the tree; one had a long thin
neck, the second had a very narrow chest, and the third had
a wooden leg. Although they may have looked different,
they shared a common trait which made them very much
alike. They were all greedy.

These three strangers soon became acquainted and began talking about the fun they were going to have at the
festival. They would win lots of money playing cards and
with it they would buy many good things to eat—wine and
smoked fish, sweetmeats, spiced eggs, curried chicken with
fine rice, guava pickles, chillies, roasted goat . . .

"Oh, this talk makes me so hungry!" interrupted the man
with the thin neck, hoping the others would offer him
something to eat. He did not want them to know he had

some popcorn in his basket; he might have to share it with them.

"Well, how do you think I feel?" whined the man with the narrow chest, cautiously fingering some hard-boiled eggs hidden under his vest. "I haven't eaten since I left my village before sunrise, and I shall have nothing to eat before I get to the mela."

The man with the wooden leg leaned against the trunk of the tree, pushing his cloth bundle of roasted soy beans behind his back as if to pillow himself more comfortably.

"Ha," he chortled, waving his wooden leg in the air. "I may not have as much to fill up as you do, but my belly groans for food. If this chowtara were a tea stall, I would buy five glasses of rockshee, a hatful of pounded rice, and an omelet with . . ."

"Stop!" cried the man with the thin neck. "I can't stand this talk any longer. Let us see if we can get a chicken from the ironsmith's house down there in the valley. We can come back here and cook it together."

His two companions agreed to this at once. So the man with the thin neck went down to the smith's to bargain for a chicken, the man with the narrow chest climbed the steep hillside to fetch wood from the forest, and the man with the wooden leg went up the trail to a shepherd's hut to borrow a cooking pot.

In a short while the three travelers returned to the chowtara and began to prepare for the feast.

The man with the thin neck built a small fire while his two companions killed the chicken and cut it up for frying. When the ghee and spices were ready, they dropped the chicken into the pot and squatted around it to watch it cook.

The smell was almost more than they could bear. Each

blew long and hard on the coals to make the wood burn faster. They took turns stirring the chicken. Finally no one spoke; all leaned forward eagerly, staring down into the pot in silence. At last the man with the thin neck lost patience.

"I must see if it is done!" he cried. He grabbed the biggest piece of chicken, flung it into his mouth, and tried to swallow it whole.

But the piece of chicken was much too big. Try as he would, he could not make it go down nor could he make it come up again. There it stuck in the middle of his throat, and he died.

"See!" the man with the narrow chest shouted to his companion. "He is finished! Now you and I will have a larger share of the chicken. What luck!" He struck his chest with such a blow of delight that he fell over dead.

The man with the wooden leg jumped up and danced about gleefully. "Tuck-a-brassi!" he shouted. "Now the luck is mine. I can have all the rest of the chicken to myself."

But as his luck would have it, he slipped on a wet leaf and fell to the ground, striking his head a mortal blow on the big flat rocks of the chowtara.

Waiting behind the peepul tree was a very patient jackal. He trotted cautiously from his hiding place, ate a delicious meal of curried chicken, licked the pot with great care, and strolled off to the mela.

Bundar Bahadur Poon 🌸🌸🌸

🌸🌸🌸🌸🌸🌸🌸 Bundar Bahadur Poon was a great nuisance to his seven uncles. He was always getting into mischief—taking their tools, playing house in their best clothes, drinking their rice wine. Even Bundar's mother complained about her son's behavior; but because she was his mother, she loved him and fed him well.

Bundar's father had been killed on the trail by a falling rock, so Bundar lived with his mother and his seven uncles and aunts on the old family farm. In many ways Bundar was much like other village boys. He laughed at silly jokes and teased the village girls. But in one way he was very different. Bundar Bahadur Poon was a monkey.

One day Bundar's uncles decided to go hunting.

"I want to go hunting, too!" shouted Bundar when he heard the news.

"No!" complained the uncles in one voice. "You will scare all the game away. Now run along and play with your friends."

Bundar disappeared as if to do their bidding, but when the uncles left the courtyard he came out from his hiding place and followed at a safe distance behind them.

Soon the uncles came to a large grove of mangoes.

"For once our monkey nephew would have been useful," laughed the eldest brother. "If he were here now, we could send him into the trees to get some good mangoes. These on the ground are all spoiled."

"Here I am!" shouted Bundar. "I will pick some good mangoes for you."

He was already in the trees, throwing down the fruit before the uncles could scold him for his disobedience. Soon he began tossing the green mangoes to his uncles and keeping the ripe ones for himself.

"Oh, what a rogue you are!" shouted the uncles, throwing the green fruit back at him. "Go home where you belong and do not follow us anymore."

Bundar leaped through the trees as fast as he could to escape the hail of green mangoes. "Ama, Ama, Ama," he cried, to make his uncles think he was running home. But when all the uncles were out of sight, he turned around and followed them again.

As it grew dark, rain started to fall. Again the hunters wished they had allowed their monkey nephew to come with them.

"He could have climbed high into a tree and searched the darkness for a light, so we would know where to look for shelter," said the youngest uncle.

"Here I am!" shouted Bundar once more, and before the uncles could recover from their surprise, Bundar was running through the trees pointing to a light across the valley.

The uncles followed Bundar's directions back and forth along the winding, slippery trail until at last they reached the door of a low stone house covered with thick wooden shingles.

"Ho!" the eldest uncle called out. "Is anybody home?"

No one answered.

The eldest uncle shouted louder this time. "Ey, Ama! Can you give us shelter for the night?"

Suddenly the door opened, and there on the porch stood a beautiful woman.

"What do you want?" she asked in a very deep voice.

The uncles looked at each other in distress. From the tone of the woman's voice they knew she was not a beautiful woman at all. She was a monster in disguise.

They whispered together for a moment, trying to decide what to do. Most of them wanted to run, but it was too late for that. It was raining very hard now and had become so dark they could only vaguely see the person in front of them. Finally, the eldest spoke again.

"We were out hunting and could not return to our home before dark, so we are looking for a place to spend the night."

"You may stay here," replied the monster woman, "if you are prepared to marry my daughters."

The uncles were afraid of this woman but when they looked back they were more afraid of the forest; bhoots and prates and other evil spirits lurked by the trail and captured people who walked after dark. So they agreed to marry the monster's daughters in return for a night's lodging.

As soon as their hostess had brought mats for Bundar and his seven uncles, so they could sit beside the fire, she turned to her daughters and said:

"The Brahman priest will be called in the morning for the wedding ceremony, so give our guests the best food and wine we have in the house and let them smoke as much as they wish."

While the men were drying their clothes and eating the meal prepared for them, the monster woman went into the back room to make the beds. This wicked creature did not intend that the uncles should marry her daughters at all. She wanted to eat the men for supper. She fixed seven beds on one side of the room, for the uncles, and seven beds on the other side, for her daughters—covering the uncles' beds with red blankets and her daughters' beds with white blankets, so she wouldn't get them mixed up. Bundar's bed was in a basket put in the corner.

While everyone was settling for the night, the monster went to bed herself, and pretended to sleep. Soon the only noise in the house was the deep breathing of people asleep. The monster was just about to get up to eat the seven brothers, when she remembered Bundar Bahadur Poon.

"Oh, Sister's Son," she whispered. "Are you asleep?"

"Yes," came the reply.

"You are not, or you could not say 'yes'," said the monster in a huff. "What do you want?"

"I'm thirsty," answered the monkey. "I want some milk to drink."

The monster was so eager for Bundar to go to sleep that she got up and warmed some milk for him. When he finished drinking it, he lay back in his basket and covered himself with his blankets.

In a few minutes the monster whispered again. "Oh, Sister's Son, are you asleep now?"

"No," was the reply.

"Why not? What do you want this time?"

"I am hungry."

"Hungry!" repeated the monster in an angry voice. "My daughters fed you chicken and rice, with wine and spiced eggs. What more do you want?"

"My uncles ate it all," whined Bundar. "I want some rice pudding."

The monster was very annoyed, but she didn't want to waken the others by arguing with the monkey, so she rose from her bed and made Bundar some rice pudding. After he had eaten it, he crawled under the covers and pretended once more to sleep.

When she was quite sure he would not answer, the monster whispered: "Are you asleep now, Sister's Son?"

"No. I can't go to sleep," was the answer.

"WHY NOT?" growled the monster.

"Because I have no popcorn. I always have to have popcorn before I go to sleep."

The monster was getting very hungry, herself. She looked longingly at the seven sleeping uncles and pictured the wonderful feast she would have if she could ever satisfy this stubborn monkey. She got up and cooked Bundar some popcorn. Climbing back into her bed again, she was so tired from all her extra work that she dozed off. Her heavy snoring rattled the brass rice spoon on the shelf.

As soon as Bundar heard her snoring, he jumped up and scampered about the room as fast as he could, putting the white blankets on his sleeping uncles and covering the monster's seven daughters with the red ones. After he had changed all the blankets he hopped back into bed and lay very still.

Suddenly the monster woman sat up with a start. She leaped out of bed and peered into Bundar's basket.

"Are you asleep at last, Sister's Son?" she whispered. This time she received no answer.

"Oh quickly!" she said to herself. "I must eat before everyone wakes up." She grabbed her kukari from the wall, ran to the beds covered with red blankets, and fell to gobbling up her daughters. "Such delicious hunters," she kept thinking with every bite. "So juicy and tender!" She was so stuffed when she finished eating her last daughter, she dropped into bed. This time she slept soundly.

Bundar jumped down from his basket and awakened his

uncles. When they heard what had happened, they ran out into the jungle and hid in a large oak tree.

In the morning, when the monster woke up and discovered her terrible mistake, she shrieked with rage. She rushed out of the house in a frenzy and started hacking at the forest wherever her kukari chanced to fall. A jaybird, calling to warn all the jungle creatures to stay in their nests, only made the monster more angry. She looked up to throw a stone at him, and there she saw the frightened uncles, clinging to the branches of the oak tree.

"Ha!" she screamed. "I have found you already. Now I will make you pay for your evil trick!" She lunged at the tree and started to chop it down. Huge chips flew everywhere. With each blow of her big kukari, the uncles were almost thrown from their perch. Suddenly, without warning, the weight of the seven men broke the tree and it fell with a great crash to the ground. The surprised monster, who had not been able to jump out of the way, was killed instantly.

The uncles cried aloud in their joy. They climbed out of the tree and ran as fast as they could back to the monster's house. There they loaded themselves with presents for their wives—all the silver jewelry and fine clothes that had belonged to the wicked monster and her seven daughters. Bundar, who took only an old drum, danced and sang at the head of the procession all the way home.

The seven aunts were delighted with their gifts, but Bundar's mother was very disappointed.

"See, Bundar Bahadur Poon, what my brothers have brought their wives," she said sadly. "And you have brought me only an old drum."

"Don't be unhappy with me, Ama," replied Bundar. "Hand me the maana measure from the storage basket."

"What have you brought that can be measured?" she asked in a pique.

"You will see," said Bundar patiently.

He gave the drum a blow on the head with his kukari, and to the mother's amazement golden coins spilled out all over the floor.

"Oh, Bundar!" cried the mother, hugging her son with joy. "What shall we do with all this money?"

"Tomorrow I will go with my uncles to the bazaar to buy rice. Would you like to eat rice the rest of your life, Ama, instead of corn?"

"Oh, yes, good son! Let us plant lots of rice," answered the mother. "I am so tired of corn."

The next morning, when Bundar's uncles were ready to go to the bazaar to buy rice, Bundar said he wanted to go with them. But they had forgotten that he had saved them from being eaten by the wicked monster. All they remembered was the nuisance he made of himself when they wanted some good mangoes.

"Oh, no!" the eldest uncle replied. "You might tell the shopkeeper we have lots of jewels. Then he would charge us more money for the rice. Go away; go and play with your drum."

Bundar went back into the house, pretending to do as he was told. But when his uncles were out of sight, he followed them to the bazaar. After they had purchased their rice seed and started home, he went into the same shop; but instead of buying rice he bought a handful of gourd seeds. When his mother saw what he had done she let out a sob.

"Oh, Bundar," she moaned. "Just when I think you are being very clever, you do something very stupid. Now, when your uncles and aunts are eating rice, what will we be eating? We cannot eat gourds!"

"Don't worry, Ama," said Bundar reassuringly. "We will have rice to eat, also. Just be patient."

The day before the uncles' rice was to be harvested, Bundar went to the rice fields and caught a big rat.

"Rat," Bundar announced, holding him at arm's length, "I am going to kill you!"

"Oh please do not kill me," pleaded the rat. "I will do anything you wish."

"Very well. I will give you a chance to save your life. If you will harvest all my uncles' rice and store it in my gourds by tomorrow morning, I will not kill you."

"Of course! That is easy," answered the rat. "Let me go and I will show you how fast it can be done."

Bundar opened his hands and the grateful rat leaped down and disappeared into the rice paddy. That night he called all of his relatives together and told them what they had to do to save his life. The next morning every grain of rice from the uncles' fields was harvested and stored in Bundar's gourds.

When Bundar showed his mother the gourds, she stared in disbelief. Her son had not plowed. He had not planted. He had even been spared the tedious job of harvesting the crop. All he had done to fill their storage bins with rice was to sprinkle a few gourd seeds on the stony ground. She never dreamed her son could be so clever.

As for the uncles, they had learned their lesson well. Never again did they go anywhere without their nephew Bundar Buhadur Poon.

And Bundar's mother never again complained of having a mischievous monkey for a son.

The Jackal and the Bear ✿✿✿

✿✿✿✿✿✿✿ Once upon a time a jackal and a bear met on a ferris wheel at a village mela. The two had a jolly time together. They pushed each other on the giant swing. They drank and gambled and laughed and joked all night. By the following morning they had become such good friends they decided to become "meets." To make this vow of friendship binding, they exchanged rupees and began to call each other "Meetju."

When it came time to part, the jackal said: "Meetju, we are like real brothers now. We must not separate. Let us live together under one roof and try our hand at farming."

The bear thought this was a good idea, so the two set out together in search of a suitable home. Some distance above the village, in the jungle where people gathered wood, they found a shepherd's hut which had been deserted for a long time. After covering the roof with a new bamboo mat to keep the hut dry, they bought a bull with the money they had won at gambling and began to clear the land.

Now the bear was a good-natured fellow who worked hard, but he was very stupid. The jackal, on the other hand, was very clever but he did not like to work at all. By the time they had finished hilling their first crop of corn together, the jackal was sure he did not like sharing the life of a farmer with a bear.

The next morning the jackal said: "Meetju, I will work in the fields now and you go out to graze the bull. In this way we will take turns and the work won't seem so dull."

The bear liked this arrangement. Every morning he would get up early and chew some parched corn and drink some beer for breakfast. Then he would climb up into the thickest part of the jungle to graze the bull. He watched the bull carefully all day long, so it would not get lost or eaten by tigers. Meanwhile, the jackal would lie in the shade all day while the corn grew.

When it was time to harvest the corn, the jackal said: "Meetju, you have worked hard and long at grazing the bull. He looks very strong. Now I will take my turn with the grazing and you can work at home in the fields."

The bear was always agreeable after a compliment, so he stayed home to harvest the corn while the jackal took the bull to graze.

The bear worked steadily all day long. The jackal was less diligent. He found it too much effort to go into the thickest part of the jungle where the grazing was good. The climb was difficult, and he had to follow the bull all the time to see that he did not get lost or eaten by a tiger. To make things easier for himself, he took the bull down the mountain to graze in the open fields. It did not matter to him that there was very little grass. The important thing was to be able to lie on the wall in the shade near the berry patch and watch the bull, without having to get up and chase him. Late in the evening, when he was sure it was too dark to help the bear harvest the corn, the jackal took the bull home.

After several weeks of this kind of treatment the bull grew very thin. And although the bear was a dull fellow, he wasn't blind.

"Meetju," he said one evening, "why is our bull getting so thin?"

The jackal was ready with an answer.

"We are not all blessed with the same gifts, Meetju. I will never be the fine herder you are," he replied with a sigh. "Wherever I have taken the bull, others have been before me—so he has had very little to eat. But today I made a great discovery! I found a place where the grass grows as high as the bull's knees. Tomorrow I will take him there and he can feast until he can eat no more."

The bear was happy to be recognized as the better herdsman so he said nothing more.

The next morning when the jackal went out to untie the bull he noticed that all the corn would be harvested by nightfall. This was the day he had been waiting for. He drove the bull up to the jungle but he did not take him to the tall grass as he had promised. Instead, he took him far up to a high, barren cliff where there was no grass at all. When the bull put his head down to chew on a small fern growing out of a rock, the jackal gave him a shove and sent him rolling over the cliff. Then he ran down the mountain as fast as he could, dragged the animal into a deep ravine where no one would see him, and sat down to his feast.

All morning the jackal ate the bull. When he had stuffed himself as much as he could, he gathered everything that was left and carried it back up the mountain to a cave in the side of the cliff. He carefully placed the meat at the back of the cave and filled the entrance with stones until there was only a small hole left, just big enough for him to enter. Then he put the bull's tail in the hole, with the end showing from the outside. When everything was arranged just as he wished, he lay down to rest. He did not move again until he was sure the bear had finished harvesting the corn.

"Well, Meetju," the bear said when he saw the jackal coming down the trail all alone, "where is the bull?"

"Oh, Meetju," whined the jackal in return. "Today I have had a terrible time. The bull got stuck in a cave and try as I would, I could not get him out. I am weak, Meetju, but you are very strong. Tomorrow, if you will go up there with me, I am sure you can get him out."

The bear, softened with flattery, could not refuse his friend's request.

The next morning the jackal took the bear to the cave. When they reached the entrance the jackal said: "Meetju, you are too big to go inside that hole. I will go in and push the bull from the inside, while you stay out here and pull from the outside. But don't pull until I tell you I am ready. When I say, 'Meetju, here he comes,' you grab the tail with both hands and pull as hard as you can."

The bear agreed to this plan and the jackal went inside the hole. He picked up his end of the tail and prepared for the pull that was to come. When he had braced himself properly, he shouted: "Meetju, here he comes!"

The bear grabbed the tail with both hands, put his feet

against the sides of the cave, and pulled with all his might. When the Jackal felt all of the bear's weight pulling against him, he let go, and the bear went tumbling over the cliff toward the river.

The jackal brushed his hands together and smiled to himself. He was delighted to think his plans had worked so successfully. The corn was all harvested, the bull did not need herding any more, and the bear would no longer be around to eat anything or complain if things did not go his way. "Now," thought the trickster, "I am free to do just as I please."

He ran down to the hut to get a basket and a kukari so he could cut up any meat that was left over and carry it home. He put some cornmeal in the basket to make his lunch complete and headed back up the mountain.

To his great surprise, there in front of the hole was the bear, sitting with his arms around his legs in a very humble manner.

"Oh, Meetju," moaned the bear as the jackal approached. "What happened to the bull?"

"You pulled much too hard," was the quick reply. "You just don't know your own strength. The bull fell into the river and drowned. He made a terrible splash!"

"Dear, dear," muttered the bear. "We will never see him again. I almost lost my life too!" Then he added, looking up at the jackal: "Why have you brought the kukari and the pack basket?"

"I decided to come up to the forest to cut some wood. I knew you would feel very sick after your fall and would not want to work. I was going to tell you to go home and rest."

This news helped to cheer up the bear. It was nice to have such a thoughtful brother, he said to himself. Then he saw the cornmeal.

"But Meetju, why did you bring the cornmeal?"

"I thought you would be very hungry after such a fall, so I brought you some food."

The bear smiled. He looked very happy.

"Oh, I have the best Meetju in the world," he cried, jumping up and hugging the jackal.

The jackal started to laugh. The bear, who thought perhaps he should be laughing, started to laugh too. Soon they were both rolling on the ground with laughter. When the brothers were too exhausted to laugh any more, they sat down on a rock together and ate the cornmeal. Then they went off to the forest to cut wood.

It is said they are still calling each other Meetju, although one cannot be sure. A stupid, hard-working bear is hardly the match for a clever, lazy jackal.

The Proud Father

❀❀❀❀❀❀❀ Dil Bahadur was a very dignified Rat with a handsome moustache and a portly bearing. He lived with his family in the grain storage room of a large Rana palace.

Dil had many children but none did he love more than his eldest daughter. When this child was born, there were so many well-placed stars in her horoscope that the Brahman had difficulty finding a suitable name for her. He counted on his fingers. He consulted his long, red book. At last he chose one name which seemed to fit the baby best— Lakshmi Devi, Goddess of Good Fortune.

Lakshmi Devi was a sweet-tempered, generous creature and she grew more beautiful as the years sped by. At last it was time for her to be married.

"I cannot marry her to just any Rat," said Dil Bahadur to his wife one day. "She is far too beautiful. In fact, I cannot marry her to a Rat at all. Not one that I know is good enough for her."

He paused to think for a moment. Then suddenly he said: "The Sun is more powerful than anything else in the world. And he is handsome, too. I shall marry her to the Sun!"

When Lakshmi Devi heard what her father had in store for her, tears came to her eyes.

"But I do not want to marry the Sun, Father," she protested gently. "I want to marry another Rat just like myself."

Dil Bahadur was very disappointed. He thought of all

the praise he would receive from everyone if he arranged such a match. It would bring great honor to the Rana family.

"Think how many girls would envy you," he said to his daughter impatiently. "Why are you so troubled? Don't you like the Sun?"

"Of course I do, Father," sobbed Lakshmi. "But . . ."

"Then the matter is settled," he announced, looking into the mirror to smooth his moustache. "I will arrange the marriage. You may be too young to appreciate it now, but when you are older and wiser you will be very glad that I chose the Sun for your husband."

He put on his English suit-coat, tucked his kukari into his cummerbund, picked up his walking stick, and strode off down the trail.

When Dil Bahadur approached the Sun's palace, he found the prospective bridegroom sitting in the courtyard smoking his hooka.

"Greetings, oh Sun," Dil said respectfully, touching his palms together and raising them to his bowed forehead. "That is a good crop of barley you have there."

"Ah, yes indeed," answered the Sun, looking across his yellow fields. "This has been a very good year for barley."

He offered Dil Bahadur a rug to sit on and after exchanging a few polite remarks with his guest, he said:

"What brings you so far from home, good friend, when the crops are almost ready to harvest?"

"Oh, Sun," began Dil Bahadur slowly. "You are the richest and most powerful in all the world!" He paused to take a sip of sweet tea that had been put before him. "Therefore, you deserve the very best for a wife. I have a daughter whose beauty far exceeds my ability to describe it. She is a goddess of delight—helpful, kind and generous.

She is worthy of the best husband I can find for her. It is a great compliment to you that I come here now to offer her hand in marriage."

The Sun's eyes betrayed a faint smile, but Dil Bahadur only noticed that he took another puff on his hooka.

"Thank you," he said finally. "I accept your most generous compliment. But I must not fail to point out to you that there are others more powerful than I, whom you should consider for such a worthy daughter. Do you realize that the Clouds are always getting in my way?" He raised his hands in a gesture of helplessness. "What can I do against them?"

Dil Bahadur could not control a sudden gasp. It had never occurred to him that anyone was more powerful than the Sun. His moustache trembled. "What shall I do now?" he thought to himself. "I do not want to offend him by withdrawing my offer, but there is no denying it, the Clouds can cover him whenever they wish. Lakshmi Devi will have to marry a Cloud."

"If you are not the most powerful one in the world, surely you are the most honorable," said Dil, regaining his composure. "When you are ready to marry, I would be happy to give you any one of my other beautiful daughters."

He finished his tea with ease, thanked the Sun for his hospitality, and hurried off to visit the Clouds.

"Where is your headman?" he asked a young Cloud. "You must show me to him; I have important business to discuss."

The young Cloud hastened to do as he was told, and soon Dil found himself in the courtyard of the Chief.

"Great Mukiya," Dil began, when it was time for him to speak of his reason for coming. "You are more powerful than anyone I have ever known. Why, you can even hide the Sun! I have a charming daughter—a gem who dazzles everyone with her beauty and grace. So many have come to ask me for her hand." He took a long, slow sip of tea, sighing loudly with contentment as he put the cup down. "But I am very particular. What would you say if I offered her to you in marriage?"

The Chief of the Clouds raised his billowy eyebrows in astonishment. He thought Dil Bahadur had come to ask him for advice.

"Why, I—I would be flattered, you can be sure," he stuttered. "But you would never forgive me if I did not tell you there is another more powerful than a Cloud." The Chief tried to look very sad. "He pushes all of us about whenever he wishes. We are always at his mercy!"

"Who is that?" asked Dil in surprise.

"The Wind."

"Well," Dil answered, "I never thought of the Wind as a proper husband for my daughter." He stared into his empty cup. "But of course," he said suddenly, jumping to his feet, "if you say she must marry the Wind, she must marry the Wind. I will see to it that she does! Yes, I certainly will!" He gave the Cloud a brisk, soldierly salute and hurried off to see the Wind.

"Wind, my friend," Dil said, as soon as it seemed proper, "you are the most powerful being in all the world. You command the greatest respect. I have a daughter whose gentle manner is surpassed only by her good looks. She is a beauty, rare and wonderful, and certainly worthy of some-one as great as you. Shall we arrange a marriage?"

The Wind gave a long sigh, to keep from laughing aloud. "I would be delighted to marry your daughter," he said finally. "At the same time I cannot deceive you. It is true that I am treated with great respect. But there is another, more powerful than I, whom I cannot bend to my will." He lowered his head as if the thought troubled him.

"Really?" asked Dil. "Who can this be?"

"The Mountain."

"Dear, dear. I did forget how powerful is the Mountain," said Dil. "Yes, you are quite right. Thank you, good Wind, for reminding me." And after swallowing his tea in great haste, he hurried off to see the Mountain.

"Honorable Mukiya," said Dil, as soon as he was seated, "no tea, thank you. I am here on urgent business. You are so powerful. You are so strong. You are so wise. None can call himself your equal. I have a very beautiful daughter who will make the most wonderful wife in all the world. You alone, deserve such a prize. Marry her and you will rejoice forever."

"Marry her and you will rejoice forever," repeated the Mountain. "Well, of course I would be honored to marry your daughter, but if you want me to marry her because I am the most powerful in all the world, then I shall have to admit there is someone else more . . ."

"Oh, no," interrupted Dil, in a tired voice. "Who can that be?"

"A Tree," said the Mountain, happy that the Rat was not going to argue over the marriage. "If the Trees were not holding me so tightly, I could travel all the way to India."

"Who would have dreamed Trees would have more power than the Mountain," moaned the bewildered Dil. "I suppose I should thank you for bringing this to my attention. I shall go to them at once." And off he ran, to visit the Trees.

"Beautiful Trees," he said, without bothering to sit down, "you are so powerful you can hold the Mountain in place. I have been searching everywhere for a husband worthy of my lovely daughter, and the search has led me to your door. If we can arrange a marriage for Lakshmi Devi with your distinguished Mukiya, you will be forever grateful to me. Such a union would brings years of the greatest joy and prosperity to all your clan."

The Trees looked at one another in disbelief.

"Is this talk coming from a Rat?" whispered a tall Tree to his neighbor. Then he turned to Dil Bahadur and asked: "Do you know who has more power than we have? Do you know who makes our lives miserable?"

"Well, no," said Dil Bahadur. "I can't imagine. Who?"

"Rats! You and your relatives. If it were not for the Rats who eat our roots and destroy our bark, we would be the most powerful creatures alive. We hate Rats! And you want our Mukiya to marry your daughter?" The Trees began to laugh.

Dil Bahadur crumpled with shame. He turned and fled. He ran far down the mountainside—away from the laughing Trees, through the corn fields, and down into the rice paddies. Only when he reached the water mill did he stop to rest.

Suddenly Dil Bahadur Rana began to puff up until his English suit-coat strained at the seams. He had never known he was so powerful. Why, he must be more powerful than anyone else in the whole, wide world!

He jumped up and rushed home as fast as his little legs could take him. When he finally caught his breath, he arranged a wedding for his daughter with another Rat; and Lakshmi Devi lived happily ever after, married to someone just like herself.

The Stolen Jewel

❀❀❀❀❀❀❀ Long ago, and far, far away in the high Himalayas of Nepal, there lived a young king and queen who were eagerly awaiting the birth of their first baby.

One day the king summoned his messenger to the drawing room. Soon after, the messenger went out to climb the highest mountain that rose up behind the palace walls. When he reached the top, the messenger raised a long copper horn to his lips, and the notes that came forth were as clear and as beautiful as any ever heard across the land. Far on the other side of the valley, another bugler waited at the top of the ridge, to send the news across the valley beyond him. In this way the birth of the baby, Prince Krishna, was announced throughout the kingdom of Jumla.

A few years later a terrible disease descended upon the little kingdom. Many people in the villages fell ill and died. Not even the walls of the castle could keep out the dreaded sickness and soon the king and queen were dead, too. All over the countryside the beloved rulers were mourned.

Now Prince Krishna should have become king when his father died, but he was still a boy so his father's younger brother was chosen to rule until Krishna was old enough to be king himself.

Things went well for a time. Then one day Krishna overheard his uncle talking.

"I like being king very much," the uncle was saying to his wife.

"I like being queen, too," she replied. "What shall we do when it is time for Krishna to be king?"

"Well, he can't be king if he is dead," laughed the uncle. His mouth twisted into a cold, crooked grin.

When Krishna heard this he became very frightened. He knew now that the greedy man and his wife wanted to kill him so that they could rule the kingdom forever.

That night Krishna went out into his father's stable. There he found some ragged clothing and an old blanket with which he disguised himself as a beggar boy. He was able to escape through the back gate of the courtyard without being detected by the palace guards.

Krishna wandered for several years over many mountains. Some nights he would sit with shepherds in front of an open fire, joking and laughing with them and sharing their roasted potatoes. During the days he would beg from the vendors in the bazaars. Often he would be so tired he would roll up in his blanket beside the trail and sleep until his hunger woke him up again.

People were very good to him wherever he went, but they did not have much time to sit and talk. They were always busy cutting fodder or chasing their goats and sheep. In his loneliness, Krishna made friends with the animals. When he talked to the monkeys, they would tell him funny stories.

They would do all kinds of tricks to make him laugh. Other animals would feed him; buffaloes would bring him milk, birds would guide him to water, and rats would bring him wheat heads from the fields. During the night fierce village dogs would lie at his side to protect him and keep him warm.

One day while Krishna was strolling in a bazaar, he saw a young girl sitting on the temple steps, weeping. She was ragged and dirty and her hair had not been combed for many days, but Krishna could see that she was very beautiful. He squatted beside her and spoke gently.

"Why is such a pretty girl crying?" he asked.

"Boke-lagyo, I am hungry," she managed to say between sobs.

After the girl had eaten some of the pounded rice Krishna offered her, she told him her story. She had been wandering for a long time, too.

"I am an orphan," she said sadly. "People call me Sumindra, but if my parents were still alive I would be called the Princess of Dang."

"How amazing!" cried Krishna, searching her face to be sure she was not deceiving him. "If my parents were alive today, I would be the Prince of Jumla."

The two orphans sat together on the steps of the temple and talked. They were so happy to find they were both children of royal blood that they decided to get married.

"Now that we have become husband and wife," said Krishna to his new bride, "we should build a house."

"But," asked Sumindra, "how shall we make a living?"

"Let us build a baati in a shady place beside the trail where travelers might want to stop and rest. We can sell them spiced tea and tobacco, and you can cook dal and rice for their evening meal if they want to stay overnight."

So together the two orphans gathered long poles for the frame of their little rest house and tied them in place with lashings of bamboo. Krishna wove mats to make a roof, while Sumindra cut tall grass from the cliffs and laced it around the sides of the hut to keep out the wind. After Krishna had built a low choola at the far end of the hut where his wife could cook, Sumindra plastered the floor with beautiful red clay. When their hostel was finished, they stood in the doorway and admired every detail of it. Finally Krishna spoke first.

"And now, my sweet Princess of Dang, I must go into town to get some food supplies and brass cups for our guests. Since you married a prince without a pice, you will have to borrow one hundred rupees for him from the moneylender."

"Ah, yes," teased Sumindra, bowing very low. "I go to borrow one hundred rupees for the noble Prince of Jumla!" And away she ran, laughing, to the moneylender.

When she returned, Krishna took the money and set off for the bazaar. He had not gone more than halfway when he heard the sharp cries of an injured dog. As he hurried toward the noise, he saw some villagers cornering the animal against a wall and beating him with sticks.

"Stop, Brothers, stop!" Krishna called, running up to the men. "What has that poor dog done to deserve such treatment?"

"He has bitten one of our friends," said the villagers. "So we are going to kill him."

"Don't do that!" pleaded Krishna, stooping to look at the quivering animal. "I will give you one hundred rupees for him."

The villagers whispered among themselves that the boy was either joking or mad.

"Where is your one hundred rupees?" said one of them suspiciously.

Krishna squatted on the ground and counted one hundred rupees into piles of ten coins each, while the men gathered round and counted aloud with him. When he lifted the dog to his shoulders they all laughed and slapped each other on the back. He could hear them counting the money again as he walked down the trail toward home.

When Sumindra saw her husband coming with a dog on his shoulders, she said:

"Where did you leave the food and the brass cups?"

"Today I had to buy this poor dog to save him from being killed," explained Krishna. "But tomorrow, after you borrow another hundred rupees from the moneylender, I will go back to the bazaar and buy our supplies."

"It will take us a long time to pay back so much money," complained Sumindra, but she did not want to argue with her new husband.

Early next morning, then, she went once more to the moneylender, borrowed one hundred rupees, and returned to give them to Krishna.

On the way to the bazaar Krishna passed a shed where the blacksmiths were making sickles for the rice harvest. Suddenly a shout went up and the ringing of the hammers stopped. Out of the shed came a cat, with all the smiths chasing after him.

"Stop! Stop!" cried Krishna, running up between the poor animal and his angry pursuers. "What has this cat done to be treated so harshly by grown-up men? Don't you know animals are your friends?"

"This cat is no friend of ours," answered one of the blacksmiths. "Any cat that eats all our butter and all our meat deserves to be killed."

"Oh, don't kill him," begged Krishna. "Give him to me. I will pay you one hundred rupees for him."

The blacksmiths thought Krishna was jesting, but when he brought out his money to count it they grabbed the bag and ran away, leaving him to catch the frightened cat and carry it home.

When Sumindra saw him coming without a basketful of supplies, she knew at once he had spent the hundred rupees for the cat.

"What kind of a husband are you?" she cried. "I borrow money for food and cups, and you bring home a dog and a cat!"

"Do not be angry," said Krishna patiently. "One of these days you will be very glad we have these animals. Go again tomorrow for the money and I will fetch our needs from the bazaar."

"What will you spend it for this time?" Sumindra asked as she left for the moneylender's the next morning. She did not want to face the inquisitive sahu with another request for one hundred rupees, but she knew that a good Nepali wife did not refuse to obey her husband. Therefore she went, once more, to do his bidding.

Krishna's next trip to the bazaar was long and hot, without an umbrella to shield him from the sun, but he did not stop along the way. "I can rest while I am buying my grain," he said to himself. Just as he was approaching the big shady peepul tree that marked the entrance to the bazaar, he saw some children teasing a crippled rat. The children, laughing and shouting, were catching the rat by the tail and throwing him up into the air. The rat was squealing for mercy.

"Stop!" called out Krishna, running up to the children. "What are you doing? Can't you hear that poor rat begging you to let him go?"

"This rat isn't as poor as you think," answered the children. "He has eaten into our father's storage baskets and stolen all of our corn. We are teaching him a lesson before we kill him."

"Do not kill him!" implored Krishna. "Here, take this money. I am sure it will buy enough corn to make up for all this little animal has stolen from you. Now run along."

The children stared in silence at the money. Then they scampered off to tell their father about the strange man they had met at the peepul tree. Krishna turned homeward, carrying the grateful rat.

When Sumindra saw him coming, this time with a rat instead of a basketful of food and cups, she could not control her anger.

"What have I married?" she wailed. "A man who buys animals that most men would throw out of the house! The dog can bark. The cat can watch the rat. But what can the rat do? All he can do is eat up our grain! What grain?" And she started to cry and laugh together.

That night Sumindra did the worst thing a Nepali wife could do to insult her husband; she did not cook him any supper. Krishna went to bed hungry.

The next morning when Krishna asked his wife to go again to the moneylender, she said:

"No, I shall not go any more. I have already borrowed three hundred rupees and we have no rice for our guests and no brass cups. Now you can go and borrow the money yourself."

Krishna did not like this answer. "If my wife does not obey me," he thought, "everyone in the village will laugh and call me a fool." He turned to Sumindra.

"Wife, if you do not go we will have no food in the

house, not even for ourselves." He looked at her for a moment, picked up his kukari, and went out into the jungle to cut wood.

Realizing the truth of her husband's words, Sumindra forced herself to go, once more, to the moneylender and borrow one hundred rupees.

When Krishna came home Sumindra did not speak to him. But she gave him the money.

This time Krishna's trip to the bazaar was interrupted by the sight of some beggars who were throwing stones at a snake.

"Stop! Stop immediately!" Krishna ordered. "What has that snake done to you?"

"Nothing," answered the beggars. "But we have to kill every snake we see to be sure we won't get bitten."

"You are wrong!" answered Krishna. "Snakes can be your best friends. Let him go and I will give you one hundred rupees."

"Ha!" laughed the beggars. "Who is stupid enough to give one hundred rupees for a snake?"

"I am!" said Krishna, and while the astonished beggars watched, he pulled out his bag of money and threw one hundred rupees all over the ground in front of them.

The beggars were scrambling about on the ground picking up the money when the snake spoke to Krishna.

"You saved my life, Good Friend, and I shall be grateful to you forever. If you go into the forest and cut a piece of hollow bamboo as long as your hand, I shall give you something to put into it."

Krishna came back from the jungle with the hollow tube of bamboo and squatted on the ground in front of the snake.

"Hold it upright so nothing will spill out of it," said the

snake. Then he rose up half his length over Krishna's outstretched hands and gently dropped a precious stone from his forehead into the bamboo cup. Krishna jumped back, astounded. The stone was so brilliant it could most certainly shine in the dark for many miles. He was overjoyed! He thanked the snake as best he could and hurried home to Sumindra.

When he came to the place where he and his wife had built their baati, he was astounded once more. There, in place of the baati, stood a beautiful golden palace.

Sumindra, dressed in the garments of a princess, came running to meet him. She was not angry this time when she saw he had no rice or brass cups. With great respect she covered her head with her shawl, bowed low in front of him, and touched his feet with her hands. Then she looked up at him and said:

"See what happened to our little resthouse, my dear husband. What did you do in the bazaar today to deserve all this?"

Krishna told her everything. She laughed and danced in circles when he showed her the brilliant jewel, and she reported all the wonderful things he would see when he went inside the palace. She begged him to forgive her for being such a stubborn wife, and she promised never to be angry or argue with him again.

"You see, my sweet princess," said Krishna, "I learned a lot about animals when I was wandering in the fields and forests. They always turn out to be your best friends."

"What you say is true of the snake, Respected Husband. But the other animals have done nothing to show their gratitude to you for saving them."

"Do not be impatient, Sumindra," he answered. "Their time for being useful will come."

So the Prince of Jumla and the Princess of Dang went into the palace together and took up housekeeping with the dog and the cat and the rat.

News spreads quickly in the mountains of Nepal, and soon visitors from great distances came to pay their respects to the owners of the golden palace. One day a servant said to Krishna:

"Sahib-ji, there is a group of important-looking men in the courtyard who wish to speak to you."

When Krishna went out into the sunshine to greet his guests, he could see they were the ruling elders from many villages for miles around. He was curious to know what they wanted, but he knew it was not polite to ask. He ordered his bearers to bring fine rugs so the gentlemen could sit and smoke before they discussed their reason for coming. Finally one of the elders said:

"Krishna Sahib, our villages in Tibrikoat have quarreled for many years because we have no one great enough to help us solve our differences. We have come to ask you to be our king."

Krishna was pleased. He thanked them all for this great honor and accepted it with the grace befitting a young man destined to rule at birth. So it was that he and Sumindra became King and Queen of Tibrikoat, reigning wisely and well for some time.

Then one day Krishna went with his chief overseer to check the flow of water running into the rice paddies just below the palace. While he was talking to one of the plowmen, he noticed a tailor coming towards him from the stream below, twirling thread onto a spindle as he walked.

"What are you doing in a rice paddy, tailor?" teased Krishna in his gentle manner.

"I have come to beg a rupee from you, Your Majesty, so the shaman will treat my sick child."

"I would gladly give you a rupee," replied Krishna. "But I have no money with me. Go to the queen, up in the palace garden, and get one from her. Tell her I sent you."

The tailor climbed to the palace gate and was led by a bearer into the presence of the queen. She was picking flowers in the garden.

"Your king has sent me to make a request," he told Sumindra, after she had asked him why he had come. "It is his wish that you give me the magic jewel."

"Oh!" said Sumindra in surprise. "I would never give the snake's jewel to anyone without the king's permission. You may wait for him to come for his morning meal. Then if he wishes, he can give it to you himself."

The tailor climbed onto the garden wall and shouted down to Krishna:

"Oh, Your Majesty, the queen will not give it to me without your permission."

"Give it to him! Give it to him!" shouted back Krishna to his wife. "He needs it for his sick baby."

So the obedient Sumindra gave the snake's jewel to the tailor without arguing, and the tailor went away.

When Krishna finished his work, he turned from the rice paddies and began to climb toward the palace. As he looked up he was stunned by what he saw. The beautiful golden palace had changed back into the small grass baati and in the doorway sat Sumindra in her old rags, weeping.

"What has happened?" cried Krishna as he ran forward.

"After you told me to give the jewel to the tailor, our beautiful palace turned back into this!" she wailed, motioning about her.

"THE JEWEL!" exclaimed Krishna in a frightened

voice. "I did not tell you to give him the jewel! I told you to give him a rupee for his sick baby!"

"You told me to give him the jewel for his sick baby!" insisted Sumindra, her voice rising.

"I never said any such thing!" shouted Krishna, and they began to argue in great anger.

The dog, the cat, and the rat came running at once to see what all the noise was about.

"Stop, stop!" they cried. "A king and queen should not quarrel. We will bring the jewel back from that wicked tailor, but you must promise you will stop this quarreling."

The king and queen felt very much ashamed. They promised not to argue again, so the dog, the cat, and the rat went out in search of the wicked tailor and the stolen jewel.

At night, when they came to the tailor's house, they found him sound asleep on a mat under the ladder that led to a loft. He was snoring loudly, with his mouth wide open. The rat whispered to the others:

"Brother Cat, sit next to the tailor's head and purr softly so he will sleep peacefully. And you, Brother Dog, lie on his feet to keep them warm. I will go upstairs and look into everything there."

So the cat purred softly in the tailor's ear and the dog lay over the tailor's feet while the rat hunted everywhere in the loft for the stolen jewel. He looked into all the wooden pots and large wooden trunks. He chewed through the storage baskets. He gnawed through all the cloth bundles that hung from the rafters or lay on the floor.

"What shall we do now?" he asked his companions in a hushed voice as he came down the ladder. "I can't find it anywhere."

"I don't know where to look," said the dog helplessly.

"Maybe he has it under his tongue," suggested the cat.

The rat thought about this possibility. Then he said: "Perhaps we should find out. I will climb back up the ladder and drop some mud into his mouth. He will choke and cough and spit upon the floor. If the jewel is under his tongue it will surely come out. Then you, Brother Cat, can grab it and we will all run away."

The dog and the cat resumed their duties while the rat ran up the ladder and dropped some mud into the tailor's mouth.

"AAAAACK!" coughed the tailor, waking up with a start. And he spit, with a violent "PHOOOO" upon the floor. Out popped the jewel, just as the rat predicted. The cat pounced on it, and in an instant he and his two companions were running as fast as they could toward home.

On the way they had to cross a river with only a narrow log for a bridge. The cat and the rat started to quarrel over who would carry the jewel.

"I have it. I will carry it," said the cat.

"But you don't like water—you might drop it," argued the rat. "I think I should carry it."

"Stop fighting," the dog interrupted. "The important thing is to get it safely back to Krishna."

So the cat kept the jewel in his mouth and the three started across the river. When they were halfway along the log, the cat became terribly frightened and in a flutter of weakness dropped the jewel into the river.

"There! What did I tell you!" wailed the rat, jumping about excitedly. "Keep your eyes on it! We'll lose it! Where is it now? Where is it?"

"Here it is!" shouted the unhappy cat. But just at that very moment a big trout slid out from under a rock and gobbled it. "Look! The fish has eaten it! Now, what to do?"

As their eyes followed the trout downstream, they saw a fisherman scoop him up in his net and toss him lightly onto the shore.

"Run, Brother Dog," the rat cried. "Play with the fisherman! Do tricks for him. Do anything to get him to give you the fish."

The dog raced down to the fisherman and jumped and played at his heels, begging for the fish. Finally the fisherman said:

"You think you would like some fish to eat, do you? Well, here!" And smiling at the joke he was about to play on the dog, he cut out the stomach of the fish and threw it high up into the air. The dog barked for joy and caught it before it hit the ground.

"You silly dog," laughed the fisherman. "I give you the worst part of the fish and you act as though it is the best. Animals are so stupid!" He laughed again.

The dog, the cat, and the rat were all laughing too, but they did not stop to let the fisherman see they were laughing at him. Nor were they going to quarrel this time over who was going to carry the jewel. They raced home as fast as they could, to deliver their prize to Krishna.

As they rounded the last bend in the trail they were greeted with a happy scene. Already the little leaf hut had been turned back into a beautiful golden palace, and at the gate stood the king and queen, waiting to greet them.

Sumindra was so happy to see the animals come home she prepared a special dinner for each of them with her own hands. As for Krishna, he was so pleased with them that he made the rat his Prime Minister, the cat his Foreign Minister, and the dog his Minister of Home Affairs. And to this day, they are still in office.

Why the Flea Hops

❀❀❀❀❀❀❀ Once, during the reign of a great king, there lived in a little blacksmith's hut, a fat louse and a very small flea. The louse stayed hidden in the smith's shirt most of the time. The flea lived in the sari of the blacksmith's wife. Whenever these two came out to talk to one another, their conversation ended in a quarrel.

"Why are we always quarreling like this?" asked the flea one day. "We like the same things to eat. We are practically brothers. Why don't we exchange rupees and become 'meets'? Then maybe we would treat each other as real brothers should."

"I would like that," said the louse, who always enjoyed company. "Then you can come to live with me in the blacksmith's shirt and we can see one another more often."

So the louse and the flea exchanged rupees and began calling each other "Meetju." That night the two brothers hid together in the blacksmith's shirt.

The next morning the master of the house hung his shirt on the wall and went out to the forge to begin his day's work. The two brothers, who had been discussing their favorite foods, began to long for some tasty rice pudding.

"But how can we make rice pudding without any rice or milk?" asked the practical louse.

"I will show you how," said the flea. "Come with me."

The flea took the louse up the mountain trail until they

came to an open pasture where animals were tethered to graze. There, inside a grass shed, was a shepherd milking one of his buffaloes.

"I will get inside the shepherd's shirt," said the flea, "and bite him as hard as I can. While he is trying to catch me, you can grab some milk and run off with it."

The plan succeeded and the two brothers were soon walking toward home with a jug full of milk.

"Now I will show you where we can get our rice," said the scheming flea. He turned down another trail that led to the house of a Brahman. There in the courtyard was the Brahman's wife, winnowing the last of the rice she was going to cook for her husband's supper.

"Look at her," whispered the flea. "A Brahmani who eats rice all the time should be very sweet. While she is trying to find me in her blouse, you take some of the rice and run."

The flea had no trouble distracting the poor Brahmani from her work. The louse quickly filled his pockets with all the rice he needed and ran toward home.

When the two meets reached their house they sat down together to cook the rice pudding. The milk bubbled and gurgled, and the rice began to swell. The louse and the flea stirred the pot often, so the milk would not stick to the bottom. They dripped some of the sweet juice into their hands between each stir and licked at it eagerly. Just as they were about to take the pot from the stove the flea suggested a plan.

"Meetju," he said, rubbing his hands together. "Why don't we have a contest. We can't eat this pudding while it is so hot. Let us go up into the forest to cut fodder while we wait for the pot to cool. The one who brings home the biggest load will get all of the pudding."

The louse immediately accepted the challenge. He was

sure he would get the bigger load because a louse is much fatter and stronger than a skinny little flea.

The two brothers gathered up their tie ropes and kukaris and went up into the jungle to cut fodder. When the louse came to a big tree full of leaves he worked steadily to cut all the branches so he could make a big load. The flea, on the other hand, cut a few twigs here and there, all the while edging away from the louse until he was out of sight. Then the flea ran back to the hut, dropped his little load on the porch, and went inside. He blew on the coals to get some light from the fire, and sat down to eat the rice pudding. When he had finished all but a little bit, he filled the bowl with mud, carefully covered it with a thin layer of pudding, and ran up into the blacksmith's shirt to hide.

Presently he heard the louse coming down the trail.

The louse smiled when he saw the little load of fodder the flea had brought back from the forest. He dropped his big load down beside it and went into the hut.

"Oh, Meetju," he called out, laughing. "You have been defeated!"

No one answered.

The louse was disappointed, but he would enjoy his victory all by himself. He sat down by the fire, stirred the coals again, and picked up the bowl of rice pudding. He was so hungry he scooped up a big lump of it with his hand and tossed it all down his throat at once.

Never was such a frantic howl heard from a louse.

"Wretched Flea, you will pay for this trick!" he shouted, throwing the bowl of mud and pudding out the door.

Since that day the tiny flea has had to change his habits. He used to walk and run like many other insects. Now he stands very still until the louse is almost upon him. Then he hops.

The King Who Rides a Tiger

PART 1 ❀❀❀❀❀❀ Once, during the reign of a great king, there lived a Brahman priest, a landlord, and a shopkeeper, who decided that their valley of Sidru had become too crowded to allow them to own all the land they desired.

"What shall I do for my sons?" said the landlord. "If I divide my holdings equally among them, there will not be enough for any one of them to make a living."

"My sons will need land, too," agreed the priest. "For here there are already too many Brahmans to make holy work profitable."

"The traders tell me that there is a beautiful valley farther north," confided the shopkeeper. "It lies in the shadow of the great Fishtail peak. Let us go there together and start life anew. There will be enough land in that valley to divide among all our sons for many generations."

So the three men packed their belongings into baskets and journeyed to the valley that lay under Fishtail peak.

On their way they met a young Magar farmer named Mana Ras who was going to the same valley. He, too, intended to clear some land and start a new farm. Now the three companions had not counted on sharing the valley with a Magar farmer. They wanted it all to themselves. But since they were not able to farm everywhere at once, they took all the land facing the south, which enjoyed the most sun, and forced Mana Ras to go across the river to the slope that faced north. This side of the valley got very little sun, but Mana Ras settled down to clear his fields, without complaint.

The fields were stony and full of roots. His crops were so sparse that his little wooden storage jar never had much corn in it. When he ate breakfast there was very little left for supper. And when he ate supper, he worried about the next morning's breakfast.

One day, after the summer monsoon, a cobra slithered into the courtyard of the priest, to beg for asylum.

"Please, Pundit-ji, hide me," she pleaded. "A mongoose is coming and I fear for my life."

"Can you not see that I am busy with my worship?" answered the Brahman, sitting with his book opened on his lap. "Should serving God be interrupted to serve a snake? Go over to the landlord and ask him to hide you."

The cobra raced to the landlord's courtyard to seek protection from the mongoose, but the zamindar was just sitting down to dinner.

"Tell her to wait until I have finished eating," the landlord said to his wife.

"But I can't wait, Zamindarni," protested the cobra. "The mongoose will be here any minute!"

"Then tell her to go to the shopkeeper," shouted the zamindar, who had overheard the cobra's remark. "And come quickly with the curry. My rice is getting cold."

The cobra turned and fled to the shopkeeper, hoping at last to find sympathy. But when the customers saw her coming they all ran from the shop.

"Do you think I would hide you in here after what you have just done to my business?" yelled the angry sahu. "Go over there across the valley," he added, waving his arm, "and get that stupid farmer to help you. He has nothing more important to do."

The trail across the valley was long and steep, but the cobra knew she would soon be caught if she wasted any more time. She whirled about and disappeared down the path toward the river.

"Oh, please," she called out to Mana Ras as she approached him. "You must help me. The mongoose is coming. Hide me! Quickly! Please!"

"Of course, but where?" asked the surprised farmer.

"Your cummerbund," she panted. "Let me crawl in there."

Mana Ras unwound the long strip of ragged cloth which circled his waist, so the cobra could crawl between the folds. Then he cautiously wound it around his waist again and went back to clearing his land.

The mongoose, in the meantime, was trailing the cobra from the priest's house to the landlord's and on to the shopkeeper's. Now he was running up the path toward Mana Ras.

"Oh, Big Brother!" he called to Mana Ras. "Have you seen a cobra come by here lately?"

"Yes, I have," answered the farmer. "But she was in a great hurry. She was traveling that way," and he pointed toward the Fishtail.

The mongoose raced past Mana Ras and disappeared into the jungle.

After a long while the cobra whispered: "How far do you think the mongoose is by now?"

"He must be at least three resting places away," answered Mana Ras.

"Then I am safe," sighed the cobra. "Unwind your cummerbund and let me come out."

When the snake dropped to the ground she turned to Mana Ras and said: "Little Brother, you were the only one in this whole valley who would save my life. The others across the river have scorned both of us, but some day they will treat you with great respect. Come now, I want to repay you for your kindness."

She led him to the top of a high mountain and there commanded him to close his eyes. When she told him to open them again, he was standing in a beautiful palace.

"This is where I live," said the cobra. "Take home anything you wish." But Mana Ras could only stand and stare about him.

"Would you like the gold and silver pots?" she asked.

"Oh, no," said Mana Ras. "If I kept them in a grass hut like mine, they would surely be stolen."

"What about the elephants or the horses?"

"They would be very nice," Mana Ras admitted. "But I am only a poor man. It would embarrass me to ride on such fine animals."

"Choose for yourself, then," said the cobra. "There must be something here that would be useful to you."

Mana Ras was silent for a moment, enchanted by all the beautiful things he had never seen before. Suddenly he spoke up.

"I would like that!" he exclaimed, pointing to a little dog sitting in the corner on a couch. "She will not eat too much and she will be good company when I am alone at night. During the day when I go to work in the fields, she can stay home and guard the hut."

"Very well," said the cobra. "If that is what you want,

take her home with you. You have chosen wisely."

Mana Ras thanked the snake and left the palace, cradling the little dog in his arms.

When he got back to his hut he was very tired. He cooked a big pot of cornmeal and ate quickly, saving a handful for his little dog. But the dog was not hungry. "Perhaps she was fed just before I left the palace," thought Mana Ras, and making a soft bed for the dog between himself and the fire, he rolled up in his blanket and went to sleep.

The next morning before going to the fields, Mana Ras tried once more to feed his dog, but again the dog would not eat.

"Maybe you are used to finer food," said Mana Ras. "But I am sure this will taste very good to you when you are hungry."

He left the food on the floor, bade the animal guard the hut well, and went out into the fields to hoe his corn.

In the evening, a short time before Mana Ras was to come home, the little dog, who had been guarding the hut, stretched and stood up. Suddenly there was a loud bark and the little dog changed into a beautiful girl. The girl looked about her. Then she stamped her foot on the ground three times. At once a delicious meal appeared beside the hearth—rice and mutton curry, with many sweets. The girl separated the food into two portions, ate her share, and set the rest aside for Mana Ras. When she heard him coming down the trail, she quickly turned herself back into the little dog and curled up by the fire as if she had been there all the time, sleeping.

Mana Ras stepped into the hut and closed the door.

"What is this?" he said aloud, looking in amazement at all the food beside the fire. He sat down and cautiously picked up each dish, tasting the food with the tip of his finger. When he discovered how delicious it was, he ate hungrily and almost finished everything before he remembered his little dog.

"Ah, my spoiled pet," he began. "At last I can offer you something worthy of your attention. See how you like this!" And he put some of the rice at the animal's feet. But the dog only raised her head, then went back to sleep.

"What a hopeless animal!" cried Mana Ras. "You will not last long in this house with such a fussy appetite. But you cannot be starving or you would eat. From now on I will let you beg for food before I waste anything more on you."

He picked up the uneaten rice and curry and dropped it into the fire. Then he rolled up in his blanket and slept.

The next morning Mana Ras ate his usual breakfast of cornmeal, left a bowl of water for the dog, and went into the jungle near his house to clear more land.

In the evening, before it was time for him to come home, the little dog again turned into a beautiful girl. And, as on the night before, the food appeared, the girl ate her share, and she changed back into the little dog again. Mana Ras could not imagine who was preparing these feasts for him. He was determined to find out.

The next morning he went to clear land again. After cutting only a few trees, he returned to a spot near his hut, where he could hide and still see through the doorway. At the usual time in the evening the little dog stood up, stretched, and—to Mana Ras' astonishment—changed into a beautiful girl. The girl stamped three times on the ground with her foot and produced a magnificent meal— fried chicken, rice, chutneys, and many vegetables. She divided the food into two portions and sat down on a mat by the fire to eat her share. While her back was turned, Mana Ras stole up to the door, leapt into the room, and grabbed her.

"Oh!" she said, jumping up and spilling her food on the floor. "Do not touch me! I've guarded your hut and fed you handsomely, and yet you called me hopeless and spoiled. Why didn't you choose the gold and silver pots or the horses and elephants? Perhaps they would have pleased you better."

Mana Ras was sorry he had spoken so harshly. But how could he have known the dog who refused to eat was really a beautiful girl?

"You must forgive me," pleaded Mana Ras. "I did not know I was speaking to you when I scolded my little dog for not eating. I only wanted the dog to eat, so she would not become ill."

Mana Ras softened the girl's heart with his arguments until she was convinced that he loved her very much. After talking together for a time, they decided to get married.

"I am just a poor farmer," said Mana Ras sadly, turning his head toward the fire. "What can I give you but a hut for a home and hard work all of your life?"

The girl stood up as though she had not heard him and stamped seven times with her foot. Slowly the little hut turned into a beautiful golden palace.

"Is there no end of surprises you have in store for me!" laughed Mana Ras in delight.

The girl gave him a bewitching glance and promptly stamped her foot again. At once the horses and elephants appeared, carrying the gold and silver pots.

Mana Ras called his new bride Indra. She was a good wife and the two were very happy living together in the golden palace.

PART 2 ✿✿✿✿✿ Not long after Indra came to live
with Mana Ras, the Brahman priest across the valley decided to make a pilgrimage to the home of the god Shiva,
who lived in the snows underneath the Fishtail. To do this
he had to pass across the land on the side of the valley that
Mana Ras had been clearing for his farm. As the priest
climbed around the corner of a hill, he was amazed to see
a golden palace in place of Mana Ras' grass hut. This discovery so unsettled him that he forgot his pilgrimage and
ran back to tell his two friends.

"Brothers!" he gasped, when he saw them talking together at the sahu's shop. "You will never guess what I
have just seen!"

"What is it?" they both asked impatiently.

"A golden palace—a golden palace on Mana Ras' farm,
with horses and elephants in the courtyard and gold and
silver pots shining through the window. And there is a
beautiful girl in the courtyard, combing her hair with a
golden comb!"

The shopkeeper and the landlord laughed.

"I would like to have some of that wine you have been
drinking lately, Pundit-ji," taunted the landlord. "Then I
could see pretty girls and golden palaces, too."

"My dear friends," said the priest, "as sure as I am a

Brahman and have not had a drop of wine since the day I was born, Mana Ras has a golden palace! Come and look for yourselves if you don't believe me!"

The shopkeeper and the landlord were curious to see just how far their Brahman friend would carry his jest, so they agreed to go with him. When they came up around the corner of the hill, they saw the priest had not been joking at all. Everything he had told them was true. They decided to go at once and tell the king.

The king listened to the three men very patiently, without believing a word they said. But he was curious. After he had dismissed them, he left the palace, disguised as a yogi, and headed straight for the farm of Mana Ras. When he arrived, indeed, there was the golden palace, just as the men had described it.

Indra had been sitting in the courtyard combing her hair when she saw the yogi coming. She recognized him immediately.

"This is no yogi, but the king himself, in disguise," she thought, and ran into the kitchen. She covered her face quickly with charcoal dust and returned to the courtyard to comb her hair.

The yogi leaned on his staff and looked over the courtyard wall.

"Oh, Little Sister!" he said. "I am very thirsty. Will you fetch me a drink?"

Indra went into the kitchen and returned with a brass cup full of buttermilk.

"Oh, that was good!" said the yogi, after he had drunk it down without stopping. "But it still has not quenched my thirst. Please bring me a jug of water."

Indra returned in a moment with the water, and handed it to the yogi. He lifted it above his lips as if to drink, but after several gulps he tossed the rest at Indra, washing the soot from her face.

"Forgive me, Little Sister," he said. "But now I know how beautiful you really are."

On the way back to his castle, the king began to envy Mana Ras very much. It did not seem right to him that such a peasant should have a golden castle and so beautiful a wife. As soon as he got home he sent his soldiers to bring Mana Ras to the palace.

When the farmer was brought before him, the king pointed to a large rooster in the courtyard and said: "Bring a cock here tomorrow to fight mine. If your cock wins you can have my wife, but if my cock wins I will have your wife. Now be gone with you!"

As Mana Ras walked back through the courtyard, on his way out of the palace, he looked once more at the rooster and was frightened by its size. It was the biggest rooster he had ever seen; and it was crowing so loud Mana Ras had to hold his ears. He returned to his own palace looking very troubled. When Indra called him to eat his dinner, he said:

"No, I am not hungry. I have a problem. I cannot eat anything tonight."

"Come!" she urged. "Problems are never solved on an empty stomach."

After Mana Ras had eaten he told his wife what was troubling him.

"You must go to bed and get a good sleep," she said. "In the morning I will give you my golden ring to take to my eldest sister, Jayti. If you show it to her she will know who you are. Then you can tell her your problem, and she will know just what to do to help you."

As soon as the sun was up, Mana Ras went down the trail to visit his wife's eldest sister. She did not know who he was, but as soon as Mana Ras showed her the golden ring, she said:

"Oh, Sister's Husband, forgive me! I did not recognize you. Come in and have something to eat."

Mana Ras started to tell her why he had come, but she interrupted him.

"Please! You must eat first. Then we can solve all your difficulties. My younger sister would never forgive me if I let you return home without feeding you."

After Mana Ras had eaten, Jayti brought a baby chick from the coop and told him to take the little bird to the castle to fight the king's rooster. Mana Ras was puzzled, but he did not want to argue with his wife's eldest sister. He left the house, muttering to himself.

"Oh, Sister-in-law, you must be mad! The big rooster will only have to step on this little thing to kill it. Then the king will claim my Indra as his wife. What have you done to me?"

When Mana Ras got home he started to complain to Indra, but she would not listen to him.

"Your king has challenged you to a contest. It is getting late. He will be very angry if you keep him waiting."

Mana Ras hurried off to the king's castle, holding the baby chick gently so he would not crush it.

When the king saw what Mana Ras had brought to fight his big rooster, he laughed out loud.

"Ho, everyone, gather round!" he shouted. "You are about to witness a great battle, but be careful you don't die from laughing!"

He ordered his rooster brought into the courtyard for the fight. Mana Ras put his little chick on the ground. It was trying so hard to peep it could hardly stand up. The big rooster was released and he strutted over to the baby chick, raising his feathers and clashing his spurs together. When he was close enough to kill his enemy, he scratched the ground several times and—with the eyes of every spectator on him—sat down. The king was mystified. He talked to the rooster, he scolded him, he begged him to attack the baby chick, but the big bird would not move. In a sudden fury, the king shouted:

"Take him from my sight! Cook him for supper! Maybe that will teach him to obey me."

Then the king turned to Mana Ras and said:

"Tomorrow you must bring a goat to fight my goat. If your goat wins the battle you may have my wife, but if my goat wins I will have your wife. Now go!"

As Mana Ras turned to leave he saw the king's goat. Such a goat he had never seen before. It was tied with a heavy chain to an iron pole; and every few minutes it would back up and ram the iron pole with all its might, shaking the whole courtyard.

That night when Indra called him to supper, Mana Ras said: "No, I cannot eat. The problem I have tonight is far greater than the one I had last night. I am not hungry."

"Come," she begged. "Food and a good night's sleep will make everything look brighter. We shall solve your problem in the morning."

When Mana Ras awoke the next day, Indra gave him her golden ring and told him to go to her second sister, Mylee, for only she knew how to help him.

When Mana Ras arrived at his sister-in-law's house, he showed her the golden ring and began to tell her his troubles.

"Come in and eat first," said Mylee, "for my sister's husband must not leave my house without eating. Then I will help you."

After Mana Ras had eaten, Mylee went out to the goat

pen and returned with a baby kid, just big enough to hop about.

"Oh, Sister-in-law," moaned Mana Ras to himself as he carried the little kid home under his arm. "How can this infant ever defeat the fierce goat I saw in the king's courtyard? You must want the king to take your sister away from me."

When Mana Ras reached his palace Indra was waiting to speed him on his way and would not listen to his protests.

"You will be late," she admonished, "and the king will not be pleased. Hurry!"

Mana Ras ran down the trail with the kid tucked inside his shirt. Once again at the castle he had to face the king's ridicule.

"What is the matter with this man? Doesn't he want to keep his beautiful wife? My goat will tear his goat to pieces."

Mana Ras put the tiny kid down on the ground and stood back, trembling, to see what would happen. When the big goat saw the kid he lowered his head, bleated fiercely, and charged. Just as he was about to toss his opponent into the air, the kid hopped to one side and the powerful billy goat rammed into the castle wall, killing himself instantly.

The king was very angry. He had been tricked twice by this farmer. He was not going to be tricked again.

"Enough of this mischief!" shouted the king. "Tomorrow you will bring me some tiger's milk before sundown or I will come to your house, myself, and carry your wife back here with me."

Mana Ras returned to Indra in despair.

"This king is determined to have you for his wife, and now he has thought of something neither you nor your sisters will be able to help me solve. I must bring him the milk of a tiger!"

"If the king asked you to make a human being, you could do that too," replied Indra. "Now come and eat your supper. Tomorrow you will visit my little sister, Konchi, and she will help you get the tiger's milk."

When Konchi saw the golden ring, she knew at once the man who needed the tiger's milk was her older sister's husband.

"Come in and rest yourself," she said. "I have just made some fresh curd and millet bread. After you have eaten, I will see what we can do about getting you some tiger's milk."

"But Konchi," protested Mana Ras, "I have no time. The king said I must return with it before sundown or he will go himself to the palace and take Indra away from me."

"Sister's Husband, you would be angry if Indra sent my husband from your door without feeding him. Now come and eat. You will have plenty of time to do the king's bidding."

When Mana Ras had finished eating, Konchi went out into the stable and returned—much to her guest's astonishment—leading a beautiful tigress.

"If you take the milk in a jug, Sister's Husband, you might spill it along the way. It is better that you take the tigress herself and milk her before the king."

Konchi tied the tigress to a post by the porch and stepped inside the house for a moment. She came out carrying a handsome saddle studded with jewels and a bridle of velvet, sewn with hundreds of tiny silver bells.

The tigress was nervous in the presence of a stranger, but as soon as Konchi placed the saddle over the animal's back, it became as docile as a lamb. Mana Ras thanked

Konchi for her help, climbed onto the tiger's back, and rode off.

Indra heard her husband coming this time, and ran out to urge him on his way. But he surprised her by shouting:

"I am very late! I have business with the king and I must not keep him waiting! I will come right back."

Mana Ras sped on to the castle. People on the trail jumped aside when they heard the bells jingling. They gazed open-mouthed at a farmer riding by on a tiger.

The king, who was waiting impatiently for sundown, heard the bells and walked up to the gate to see who was coming.

"Someone must have a very fast horse," he said to the gatekeeper. When he saw it was Mana Ras riding on a tiger and heading straight for the castle, he became frightened.

"Never mind!" he shouted, waving his arms to ward off the beast. "You can keep your wife and I will keep mine!"

But Mana Ras was not to be turned away so easily. He rode up to the terrified king, sprayed his beautiful robes with milk, turned the tigress around, and galloped home.

News spread quickly of the simple farmer boy who had met the king's challenge. Soon everyone was saying:

"We need a king who is brave and who will not make trouble for the poor. Mana Ras should wear the crown."

So the old king was chased out of the valley and the throne was prepared for Mana Ras. Many people came to the coronation, with gifts to pay homage to their new ruler. Among them Mana Ras recognized the priest, the landlord, and the shopkeeper, all dressed in their finest clothes and bowing low before him.

Never before had there been a wiser king than Mana Ras, and never since has there been a king brave enough to visit his subjects riding on a tiger.

Why the Jackal Howls ✸✸✸

✸✸✸✸✸✸✸ Long, long ago, when the lake left the valley of Kathmandu, there lived in a rhododendron forest a jackal and a bulbul bird. These two animals were not fond of each other but they roamed about in the same forest and they often met while searching for food.

One day the jackal said to himself, "If I become a 'meet' to that bulbul bird, I will have a good excuse to follow him about all day. Then when the hunting is poor and I can find nothing else to eat, I can have my little 'brother' for dinner." He laughed aloud at his own cunning.

The next time the jackal saw the bulbul bird, he called out in a voice full of feigned affection:

"Oh, little bulbul, you work too hard. Come down here where it is easy to pick up the seeds that have fallen to the ground." Then he added: "It is a pity two gentlemen of such good taste do not see each other more often. We should become meets and dedicate ourselves to sharing the finer things of the forest together. What do you say to that, my friend?"

Now the bulbul was sure he did not want to become a "brother" to jackal. But to refuse such an offer would be an insult the jackal would never forget, and to be eaten by a jackal was not a very pleasant prospect.

"I am flattered that you should want me for a meet," answered the bulbul, without emotion. "Of course I can do nothing but accept."

So the jackal and the bulbul exchanged silver rupees to consummate their brotherhood and began immediately to call each other by the respectful title of "Meetju."

"Now, Meetju," began the jackal, whose mind was never at rest when he wanted something, "our life in the forest is hard enough. We must help one another as much as we can. As long as we are meets, why don't we build a house and live in it together as real brothers should?"

"This," thought the bulbul, "is going too far!"

"What kind of a house would it be? I would die if I had to live in a den," said the bulbul, giving the jackal something to think about. "And you would certainly not enjoy trying to keep house in a nest! Perhaps we should compromise. You build a den to suit your needs on the ground and I will build my nest in a tree above it. In that way we can still look out for each other."

"Good!" said the jackal, satisfied for the moment that he would always know where to find the bulbul. "You are such an intelligent fellow. But that, after all, is why I am proud to call you Meetju!"

He tried to make his smile look very sincere, yet all the bulbul could see were the jackal's two long rows of shiny white teeth.

The two meets finished building their living quarters by nightfall. They had planned to go hunting the next day, but when the jackal was getting out of bed, he found that the bulbul was up and ready to leave.

"Oh, Meetju," called the jackal. "Where are you going

today? I will join you when I have finished my breakfast."

"I am going to the east side of the river," the bulbul called back. "See you there!" And off he flew into the forest.

As soon as the jackal had eaten his cornmeal mush he went to the east side of the river to find the bulbul bird. But he could not find him anywhere. He searched until sundown without catching anything good to eat. That night he was so exhausted he settled for a supper of cold cornmeal mush and went unhappily to bed.

The next morning the bulbul again was up and ready to go to the forest long before the jackal.

"Where are you going today, Meetju?" the jackal called out after the bulbul bird.

"I am going to the west side of the river, Brother Dear," the bulbul shouted back. "Come along when you are ready!" And he disappeared into the jungle.

The jackal hunted all day long for the bulbul on the west side of the river, but he had no more luck this time than he did the day before.

The next morning when he heard the bulbul getting ready to leave, he raised himself up from the bed and called out: "Oh, Little Brother! Where are you off to, today?"

"I think I shall go back to the east side of the river again," answered the bulbul. "The hunting is excellent there. Why don't you join me?" And off he flew, without waiting for an answer.

"This time I will!" shouted the jackal, lying back on his bed. Then he added to himself: "And this time the hunting will be excellent!"

By now the jackal knew that the bulbul was deceiving him. If the bulbul said he was going to the east side of the river, he would surely be flying to the opposite side. The jackal got out of bed with great determination and went not to the east side of the river but to the west side. There he found the bulbul bird on the ground, eating berries.

Out of the bushes jumped the jackal, shouting:

"Little Brother, I will eat you now for deceiving me!"

But the nimble bird was too quick for the jackal. Up he flew, into the berry bush—the jackal's jaws snapping the air behind him.

"Oh, Meetju, you are right!" admitted the bird quickly, to the great surprise of the angry jackal. "I have deceived you and that is the very worst thing anyone could do to his beloved meet." His voice was full of penitence. "For punishment I deserve to be eaten, but it would make my next life easier if I give myself up rather than allow you to catch me. You will gain great favor with the Gods, yourself, if you grant me this last, small request. Open your mouth and I will fly in. But be sure to close your eyes, because I cannot bear to have you see me die this way."

The obliging jackal sat on his haunches, closed his eyes, and opened his mouth as wide as possible. But the bulbul bird, instead of plunging to his death, picked a big cluster of sour berries from the bush, flew over the jackal's mouth, and dropped them in. The jackal gagged on the sour berries; his body doubled up as he coughed and choked.

When the bulbul looked back and saw the success of his little trick he laughed so hard his eyes turned red, and they have been red ever since.

The jackal, who was never able to catch his Meetju, howled at his own helplessness. He can still be heard howling on a warm, dark night.

Lato, the Stupid One ❀❀❀

❀❀❀❀❀❀❀ Once, during the reign of a great king, there lived a hill man and his wife in the high, narrow valley cut by the beautiful Chimpuk River.

The couple had three sons. The eldest boy was called Jayta, the second boy was called Myla, and the third was called Koncha.

But poor Koncha was not called that for very long. Born under the sign of Pisces, the fish, he never seemed to learn how to do farm work; all he could do well was swim. When he was supposed to plow, the bullocks would get tangled in their harness. When it was his turn to graze the cattle, one of the cows would eat a poisonous plant or fall over a cliff. When he was sent to bring a load of fodder down from the forest, he would drop half of it along the way. Some of these things Koncha could not help, but one day he did something more foolish than usual; he traded his good kukari for an old pair of shoes.

"You are stupid!" shouted his angry father. "You are Lato!"

And Lato he was called from that time on.

When Jayta and Myla grew old enough to be married, their parents gave them each a beautiful bride. But when it was Lato's turn, the father said:

"This stupid boy must learn something besides how to play with fish. If he cannot take care of himself, how will he be able to take care of a wife? Instead of a bride, I will give him an old bullock and a hut up in the jungle. Maybe then he will learn how to be useful."

Lato's hut was near a trail used by many Tibetan traders traveling with their long lines of belled ponies between Lhasa and Kathmandu. Near the foot of the valley was another hut much like Lato's, but this one was known to most of the traders as a den of thieves. Here there lived a father and seven sons who captured any traveler they could find and robbed him of all his belongings.

One night, when the thieves could find no traders to rob, they decided to steal Lato's bullock.

"He will think a Tibetan stole it," said the father to his sons.

When Lato awoke the next morning he discovered his bullock was missing. He knew he had tied it securely the night before, so it could not have wandered away. He hunted everywhere, but it was not to be found. Finally he went to his eldest brother and said:

"Jayta, my bullock must have been stolen last night. I cannot find him anywhere. It is not possible to farm without a bullock, so I will have to buy another one. Will you lend me two hundred rupees?"

Jayta laughed. "If you have lost that crippled old bullock, why would you not lose another one? Besides, you could never get enough money to pay me back. Ask Myla. Perhaps he will lend it to you."

When Lato asked Myla for two hundred rupees, Myla laughed too. "What good is a bullock to you, anyway?" he asked scornfully. "You will never make a farmer. Why don't you build a hut down by the river and fish for a living? Lending money to you would be the same as throwing it away."

When Lato saw that his brothers were not going to help him, he knew he would have to borrow from the money-lender. On his way to the village he passed the hut of the thieves and there, under the cattle shed, he saw his old bullock. Lato pretended not to notice. He walked quickly on to the village and, after borrowing two hundred rupees from the moneylender, he went to a cloth shop in the bazaar. Here, for one hundred rupees, he bought a sari, a blouse, a woman's cummerbund, a pair of women's sandals, and a string of beads. With the rest of his money he bought a dhoti, a man's shirt, a velvet vest, a man's cummerbund, a new topi, and a beautiful pair of shoes.

When he returned to his hut, he dressed himself very carefully in the woman's clothing and went down the trail to visit the thieves. They were all in the house eating their dinner.

"Oh, Brothers!" shouted Lato. "If there is a fierce dog in your yard, come out and tie him. I want to go by."

"Oh! Did you hear that Tibetan?" said the father. "Quickly! Run out and catch him before he gets away."

The seven brothers gathered up their kukaris and ran outside to rob the trader, but when they saw the trader was a girl they changed their minds.

"We should not steal from such a pretty creature," said the oldest brother. "One of us should marry her instead!"

"Yes! Yes!" they agreed in unison. "But which one?"

"She's mine!" said the second brother. "I saw her first."

"But," protested the eldest, "you can't get married ahead of me!"

They all began to argue and shout at each other. Finally

the youngest brother said: "Why don't we show her to Father and let him decide?"

So the seven brothers took Lato inside the house and asked their father to settle the dispute. When the old man saw a pretty girl standing before him, he was very pleased. He said to his sons: "There are seven of you. If Jayta marries her, Myla will be unhappy. If Myla marries her, Syla will be unhappy. Our house will be divided. Since there is only one of me, it is better that I marry her. Then we will have no arguments."

After some discussion the brothers agreed, and Lato was given to the father as a bride.

Later in the day the brothers went out in search of another traveler to rob, and Lato was left alone in the house with the old thief.

"You are old and I am very young," said the bride to her new husband. "What would happen to me if you should get sick and die? Don't you think it would be better for me if I married one of your sons?"

"Oh, no!" said the old man. "That would not be good at all. Come with me and I will show you how well I have prepared for my wife if I should die."

He took his bride into the back room of the house and showed her seven large water jugs filled with silver coins.

"Oh, I am lucky!" said Lato. "I have found a husband who is as generous as he is wealthy. Come and lie down on the mat so that I can rub your back and legs with mustard oil. It will make you feel so much better."

The old thief was happy to discover he had a bride who would give him the attention a husband deserved. He lay face down on the mat so Lato could rub him with oil.

"Your skin has so many wrinkles in it, I am having trouble," said Lato after a few minutes. "It should be stretched so I can rub it more easily."

The husband agreed.

So Lato pounded four stakes in a wide circle around the old man's body and tied one limb firmly to each stake. Then he stood up and said in an angry voice: "Husband, don't think you can fool me! I know you are not a generous old man. You are a wicked old thief. You stole my bullock and I am going to give you a rubbing that you will never forget!"

He pounced on the old man and rubbed him so hard he broke three of his ribs.

Then he ran into the back room, grabbed the seven jars of coins, and rushed out into the jungle. There he buried the jars quickly and hurried home to his hut.

When the seven sons came back late that night, they found their father on the floor, in agony.

"What has happened to you?" they cried. "Where is your new wife?"

"What new wife?" moaned the old thief. "The girl you left for my new wife was Lato, the stupid one, and he has broken three of my ribs."

The brothers were furious but they were too tired to chase after Lato at that hour. They swore they would catch him the next day and kill him.

Early in the morning, while the thieves were still asleep, Lato dressed himself in the man's clothing he had bought in the bazaar and hurried down the trail once more, to visit the thieves.

"Oh, Brothers!" he called out in a loud voice. "If there is a fierce dog in your yard, come out and tie him. I must go by."

"Quickly!" said the father to his sleepy sons. "There is that stupid boy! Do not be fooled this time by the woman's clothing he wears. Put an end to him!"

The sons jumped up, grabbed their kukaris, and raced out of the house to kill Lato.

But instead of Lato dressed as a woman, they found a well-dressed man. They were surprised. The eldest brother said: "This man is not Lato, but maybe we should kill him just the same. He must have money in the bag he carries if he wears such fancy clothes."

"Oh, don't kill me!" said Lato. "I am a doctor. I can cure broken bones and bruises and a great number of ills. If any of you are sick, I will be glad to treat you."

The brothers could not believe their good fortune.

"Yes, come!" said the eldest, who always spoke for the others. "You must see our father. He has fallen and broken three of his ribs. Maybe you can help him."

When Lato went into the house, the old thief was lying on the floor, moaning in pain.

"We were just going out," said the eldest brother to Lato. "But if you need any medicine, tell us now so we can get it for you."

"No, I have all the medicine I need right here in my bag," answered Lato, patting the cloth satchel he had brought with him.

So the brothers went off to steal what they could from helpless travelers, and the doctor was left alone with his patient.

"In order to fix your ribs and make you more comfortable I will have to wrap you in a tight binding," said Lato.

"Do what you will as quickly as possible," came the muffled reply. "I can hardly breathe."

Lato rolled the old thief in a quilt and tied him round and round with the long rope that he took from his satchel. Then he pounded four stakes in a large circle and fastened his patient securely to them.

"Now, don't you feel better?" he asked.

"Oh, yes, yes," answered the thief. "This is much more comfortable."

"Good," said the doctor, standing up. "And I will be happy if you stay that way the rest of your life. Now I am going to take home the bullock you stole from me."

Lato ran out into the cattle shed to free his bullock. He dug up the seven jars of coins he had buried in the jungle, loaded them onto the animal's back, and drove him home.

When the seven brothers returned late that night, they saw their poor father tied to the ground, unable to move.

"Is this the treatment the doctor prescribed?" they asked him in surprise.

"Doctor!" snapped the father. "Do you think the man you left here with me was a doctor? This time that stupid boy has gone back up the mountain and taken his bullock with him."

The brothers saw they had been tricked again by Lato and they were infuriated. But by the time they had untied their father, they were so tired they dropped to the floor in their blankets and fell asleep.

Early in the morning, before the sun was up, they were awakened by someone shouting underneath their window.

"Ho, you good-for-nothings in there! I am Lato! Come out if you are anything but cowards, and catch me if you can!"

In spite of his broken ribs, the old man was on his feet and out the door, while his sons were still stumbling around in the dark, looking for their kukaris. But they did not tarry long. Soon they were all racing down the trail after Lato.

Lato was wearing only a small cloth around his waist so

he could run very fast. He ran all the way to the river's edge and dived in. As the thieves approached the bank of the river, Lato stood up in the shallow water and called back at them: "Come on, you clumsy bullocks, can't you plow any faster than that?"

The thieves were so angry they ran right into the river after Lato, shouting curses and flailing their kukaris. Suddenly they found themselves in the deep channel, but it was too late to turn back.

"Help! Help!" shouted the father, as the current carried him swiftly downstream.

"Help!" all the sons shouted. "We are drowning!"

The only one who could swim well enough to save them was Lato, and Lato had vanished; he was playing with his friends, the fish, in a quiet pool far below the surface of the water.

Several hours later, Lato walked up to the door of his little hut and looked about him.

"I will use some of my money to build a bungalow," he said aloud. "And it will be the finest bungalow in the Valley of Chimpuk."

The next day Lato hired the most skillful carpenters he could find, and within a few days the bungalow was finished.

Soon the news of Lato's beautiful bungalow reached the ears of his eldest brother, Jayta. "How is this possible?" said Jayta. "My stupid brother has no money. He cannot even buy a bullock."

But he went up into the jungle where Lato lived to see for himself. There, in place of his brother's hut was a beautiful bungalow, with cattle sheds and sheep pens, just as they had been described to him.

"Oh, Lato," said Jayta, as he came up to the porch where

his brother was sitting. "This is a very fine house. Now that you are a rich man you can lend me some money. I need to buy a buffalo."

"If you had given me two hundred rupees when my bullock was stolen, I would be giving you four hundred rupees in return," answered Lato. "But now I will give you nothing. If you need money you can come tomorrow to clear my land and I will pay you for your services."

By this time the news of Lato's fine bungalow had reached his second brother, Myla.

"I don't believe it," said Myla to his neighbor's son. "My stupid brother would rather live in the river than in a bungalow."

But to satisfy his curiosity, Myla climbed the steep hillside to his brother's little farm in the jungle. He stopped in awe, when he saw the new house and sheds, and Jayta working nearby, clearing the land.

Myla could not hide his surprise.

"Oh, Lato!" he called to his younger brother, who was standing in the courtyard. "What is this you have done? If you can build such a house, you can surely help your poor brother. I need two hundred rupees to buy some rice land. Will you lend it to me?"

"If you had given me two hundred rupees when I needed them to buy a bullock, I would have given you double in return. Now I will give you nothing. But you may come tomorrow to herd my sheep and I will pay you wages."

So it was that Lato, the stupid one, learned how to take care of himself. His brothers became his servants and worked for him the rest of their lives. His father married him to the most beautiful girl in the valley. And from that day on, all the villagers called him Koncha. No one ever called him Lato again.

The Soldier's Return ✿✿✿

✿✿✿✿✿✿✿ Once, during the reign of a great king, there lived a wise old man named Mudoo, with three beautiful daughters. When his wife died, Mudoo's relatives tried to encourage him to seek another mother for his children, but he preferred to raise the girls all by himself. Everyone in Doti said he was a good father.

One day Mudoo came in from the fields feeling very sick. He lay down on a grass mat in the shaded courtyard and called to his eldest daughter:

"Oh, Jayti! I am feeling sick. Get me some water to drink."

"There is no fresh water in the jug, Ba," answered Jayti from inside the house. "But I will bring some from the spring right away."

She came down the porch steps with the jug in the carrying basket, and walked quickly down the trail to the pondayra. When she put her jar under the small trough that came from the pool, she noticed the water had been muddied by a frog.

"Why did you do that just as I was coming?" she asked the frog crossly. "My father needs clear water to drink, because he is very ill. Now go away!"

"I will," answered the frog, "if you are ready to marry me."

"Marry you!" laughed Jayti. "Don't be silly! Who would marry a frog? If I have to do that, I will take the water just as it is."

She filled her jar with the water and carried it home to her father. Mudoo drank a little, but it did not taste good at all. After a while he called to his second daughter:

"Oh, Mylee! Come out a minute."

"What is it, Ba?" asked Mylee, as she hurried to him.

"The water your sister got at the pondayra seems to be dirty. Do you think you could get me some water that is clear?"

"Yes, Ba. I will get some right away," answered Mylee.

She ran back into the house for the basket and jug and hurried down the trail to the spring. When she was about to put the water jar under the trough, she heard a big splash in front of her. Looking up into the pool fed by the spring, she saw a frog swimming about, stirring up the water.

"See what you have done!" she cried out to the frog. "My father has asked me to get him a drink of clear water. Now you've made it dirty."

"I will give you clear water if you promise to marry me," answered the frog.

"Marry you!" shouted Mylee. "That would be ridiculous!"

"Then I shall not give you any clear water," said the

frog, resuming his swim.

"Don't then!" said Mylee, crossly. "I will have to go back without it."

When Mylee returned to the courtyard, she said to her father:

"There was a big frog in the pondayra, Ba. He kept stirring up the water so it would not run clear. I could not get any good enough to drink."

After Mylee had gone into the house, Mudoo called to his youngest daughter, Konchi. When Konchi saw how feverish her father was, she said:

"Don't worry, Ba. I will get you some clear, sweet water so you can drink all you wish."

She slung the basket over her back and ran down the trail to fill the water jar. As she approached the spring, a big frog jumped into the pool above the trough and began kicking vigorously.

"Oh, please!" she called politely. "Wait until I have filled my jug before you take your swim. I need some clear water for my poor father who is sick with a fever, and very thirsty."

"I will give you some clear water for your father if you will promise to marry me," said the frog.

Konchi looked at the frog in wonder. "Must I really promise to marry you before you will grant such a simple request?"

"Yes, you must," answered the frog gently. "But don't be afraid. We will be very happy together."

Konchi stood with the empty jug in her hand, watching the frog swim about. She thought of her sick father lying in the courtyard, waiting for a drink of cool water. After a moment she said:

"I must have some clear water for my poor Ba, so I will

promise to marry you."

The frog was delighted. He hopped out of the spring and the water cleared in an instant. Konchi filled her jug to overflowing, lifted it into the basket, and returned home to her father.

"Oh thank you, little Konchi," sighed Mudoo after he had finished drinking all the water he craved. "That tasted so good!" He touched her cheek in an affectionate caress. "But what is this, my child? You are crying!"

Konchi told her father everything that had happened at the pondayra.

"And I promised to marry him, Ba," she continued; "so he would give me the clear water. Now what shall I do?"

Mudoo lay back on the mat in silence and did not speak for a long time. Then he said, "Konchi, you are my dearest daughter and I love you very much. I would be happy if you stayed here at home with me the rest of my life. But you have made a promise and you must keep it. Go now, with my blessings, to marry the frog. I will trust to fate that he will be good to you."

Konchi gathered a few belongings into a basket. Through tears, she bade farewell to her father and sisters and set off, once more, for the spring.

"I am ready to marry you now," she said to the frog who was lying on the surface of the water.

"Good!" he answered, looking at her with his big, round eyes. "You have made me very happy. Follow me and I will take you to my home."

He jumped out of the pool and started hopping down the trail—phutuk, phutuk, phutuk—with Konchi following close behind him. On the way they saw many fat cows grazing in the jungle.

"These are my cows," announced the frog to his new

bride. "Do you like them?"

"But you are a frog!" answered Konchi in surprise.
"Frogs do not keep cows!"

"Oh, but I do!" said the frog. "And I will show you
something else." He hopped along the trail a little faster.

"These are my buffaloes," he said, pointing to a beautiful
herd of black buffaloes in an open field.

A little farther along he said, "And these are my sheep."

"Do you think it is right to tease me this way?" protested
Konchi.

"Oh my dear," said the frog, looking concerned. "I did
not mean to upset you. Sit down here a minute and wait
for me. I shall not be gone long."

Konchi saw that the frog was about to jump into a little
hole beside the trail.

"You are not going to leave me all alone out here, are
you? It is not right for husbands to go somewhere unless
their wives can go too."

"Do not be afraid," said the frog. "A husband goes to join
the Army without his wife, doesn't he? I will come right
back."

Konchi finally consented and the frog disappeared
quickly down the hole. As soon as he was gone, Konchi
began to feel drowsy. She lay down in the leaves to wait for
his return and fell fast asleep. When she awoke she found
herself in a beautiful palace. She blinked her eyes, thinking this was a dream. Her husband, the frog, was standing
by her side.

"This is my home, Konchi," he said in a kindly voice. "I
live here with my sister and stepmother, who are very
anxious to meet you."

He took his bride into the dining room and there sat a
very old woman and a young girl. The stepmother's stern

face frightened Konchi. But the frog's sister, Dilmana, was beautiful. She seemed delighted to have another girl her age in the palace to keep her company. After a few days, Konchi felt quite at home. From early morning to late at night, she and Dilmana could be seen working and playing together.

One day when they were in the garden picking flowers, Konchi heard the clear notes of a flute.

"Listen to that, Dilmana!" she exclaimed, standing up and looking about her. "Have you ever heard such sweet music? Who can be playing that flute so beautifully?"

"I cannot say," answered her companion, pretending not to show interest.

Konchi was determined to find out. She dashed in and out among the flowers and tall shrubs, searching everywhere for the source of the beautiful music. Suddenly she saw the flute player sitting in the palace window. He was young and very handsome. He played the long, sad notes with his eyes closed, not aware of anyone watching him.

"I saw him!" cried Konchi in breathless excitement as she ran back to her friend. "Who is he, Dilmana? Tell me if you know."

"He must be a guest who came to stay overnight," answered Dilmana.

But Konchi was not convinced. Led by the music, she ran quickly out of the garden, across the courtyard, and into the palace, to the room where the flute player sat in the window. She peeked through the long drapes that hung over the doorway so that she would not disturb him. He was indeed handsome, and dressed like a prince. The light from the hearth fire danced on his silver jacket. But what was that on the floor? Konchi stared. It was the skin of a frog! She knew at once that the boy playing the flute was her husband. She darted into the room, picked up the frog skin, and raced with it to the fire. The startled flute player jumped down from the window and dashed after her. When the boy reached the hearth, the skin was already in flames. He jabbed at it with his flute. As the two struggled, the girl trying to destroy the frog skin and the boy trying to save it, they were both severely burned on their hands. Finally, with a cry of despair, the boy gave up. The last of the frog skin turned to smoke and ashes.

"Oh, my sweet Konchi," said the handsome prince. "You are both my sorrow and my joy. My stepmother is a witch. She cursed me with that frog skin for nine hundred days, and though I could leave the spring if someone promised to marry me, I was never to be seen as a prince by my bride until the curse had passed. Who knows what a terrible punishment she will invent if she catches me now without the skin." He looked into Konchi's frightened eyes. "Come, let us hide and I will think of something to do."

The prince and Konchi hid in the palace together for two days. When Konchi awoke on the third morning, the prince had disappeared. She searched everywhere. Dilmana did not know what had happened to her brother. The two girls could do nothing but sit and weep together, to comfort one another.

The stepmother blamed Konchi for the disappearance of the prince, and as the days wore on, she became rude and harsh toward Konchi. One evening she said:

"You are not needed here anymore. Your husband has gone. You can go too. Go now, before I lose my patience."

Konchi was so afraid of the stepmother she fled from the palace without stopping to take any food. She did not know where to go. She knew she could not find her way back home. For a long time she wandered in the forest, living on berries and watercress. At night she slept in the shelter of a hollow log.

One day, during her search for something to eat, she came upon an old man, squatting near a fire in front of a shepherd's hut. His head and shoulders were covered with a blanket. Konchi could not see his face but she could tell he was weeping. She spoke gently to him and asked him what was the matter. He told her his son had died, falling from a tree, and he had no one to help tend his sheep.

"Almost every night," the old man said, "I lose another animal to a leopard."

"Do not weep, Grandfather," said Konchi, happy to talk with someone. "My husband has disappeared and I have been turned out of the house by his wicked stepmother. I cannot find my own family. Since I have no place to go, I will be glad to stay with you and help you herd your sheep."

The old man treated Konchi like his own daughter. He gave her what he could, but he was very poor. As the years passed, Konchi grew thinner and thinner and her sari was reduced to rags.

One day, while she was grazing the sheep near a chowtara, she saw a soldier coming home on leave. By his uniform she could tell he was a member of the King's Royal Guards. He was carrying, for his family, a basket full of presents that he had bought in Kashmir. When he reached the chowtara, he put his load down on the platform step and climbed onto the big terrace to sit in the shade. As he pulled an orange from his pocket, he looked up and saw Konchi staring at him.

"Oh, Younger Sister," he called politely. "Come over and share this orange with me."

Konchi shook her head. She knew it was not polite to refuse food offered by a soldier coming home on furlough, but she felt she was too ragged to sit beside a handsome, well-dressed officer.

"Come!" he pleaded.

She wandered slowly towards the chowtara, whistling to her sheep, pretending they were getting into trouble. When she was closer he said quietly:

"What kind of a Nepali girl are you? I have been away from home for a long time. The least you can do to welcome me back is to sit and share this bit of fruit. Then I will go on my way."

Konchi felt she had offended the soldier and she was sorry. She climbed onto the chowtara and sat down under the tree beside him. When he offered her a piece of the orange she noticed, with a start, that his hands had been badly burned in a fire. At the same moment, the soldier saw the scars on the hands of the shepherdess. Slowly the two began to realize that they were man and wife.

Konchi flung herself at her husband's feet, weeping and laughing. The prince could not speak for a long time. Finally he asked Konchi what had brought her to such a wretched state, and she told him all that had happened since the day he disappeared in the palace.

"Now I am a shepherdess," she continued. "And it is time for me to take the sheep back to the fold. The old man needs me. He cannot tend his flock alone and he has no one else to help him. You can easily find another girl who will make you a good wife."

"But you are my wife," said the prince. "Do not worry about the old man and his sheep. I will arrange everything to make him happy. Come with me now, back to the palace."

"But what about your stepmother?" asked Konchi. "I am afraid of what she will do to both of us."

"You need not fear her any more," said the prince, fingering an amulet around his neck. "When I was in Kathmandu, I met the shaman of the maharaj. I told him my story and he gave me a powerful spell. My stepmother's strength will be nothing now, against his. Come!"

When the couple approached their home, they saw the old woman sitting with her back to the courtyard wall, twirling wool onto a spindle. At the sight of his step-mother, the prince grew very angry. He hid Konchi near the trail and stepped out into the sunlight.

"Ey, old witch," he shouted. "Your frog has come home. Now it is your turn to go. Be off with you and don't ever let me see you again!"

The stepmother whirled around in surprise and fixed her eyes squarely on her stepson. "I have been waiting for this day," she screamed. "How dare you talk to me that way! Why, I will turn you into a frog for the rest . . ."

But the prince was too quick for her. His hand shot up to his amulet and held it tight. The old woman gave a shriek of dismay and stood still, quivering. Then, as the prince repeated his spell, the stepmother grew smaller and smaller and smaller, until, at last, she could not be seen at all. A tiny green fly, left standing in the place where the witch disappeared, rubbed her glossy wings together and flew away.

Dilmana rejoiced that her brother had come home and had rid the palace of their wicked stepmother.

The prince gave the old shepherd a flock of the finest lambs, wages for a shepherd boy, and a cottage nearby so he could come to visit Konchi whenever he wished. Dilmana married a handsome raja from another kingdom. And the prince and Konchi, together at last, reigned happily and wisely forevermore.

Notes on the Stories

✿✿✿ Patricia Hitchcock's love for folk tales grows from her interest in the people who tell them and their culture. As she says: "Folk tales reveal so much of what people think of themselves and how they view the world about them."

A young Magar high school teacher, Hem Bahadur Thapa, lived with the Hitchcock family during their stay in a Nepalese village near Tibet. Hem was one of the few hill people who knew English well and also spoke Hindi, Nepali, and his own Magarkura. Because of her friendship with Hem, Mrs. Hitchcock learned much about his people that was unknown to the world beyond the Himalayas. Climbing the trails together, they shared songs, riddles, stories, and soon became absorbed in collecting tales the Magars told their children. It was Hem who ferreted out the best of the local storytellers and, with his remarkable memory for detail, his talent for mannerisms and phrasing, translated these stories to Mrs. Hitchcock who wrote them down verbatim. Her ability to write with love and insight about the Nepalese people, their attitudes and their beliefs, has produced stories that are true to the spirit of the original telling; stories that are still being told to the children in Bhuji Khola, Nepal.

Soonimaya

In Nepal, young men often go into the army to free themselves, or their fathers, of debt. When a father goes into the army, life becomes more difficult for the mother at home. She must farm the land, herd the animals, gather fodder, and raise the children without the help of her husband. The life of a little girl may change also, because she must bear more of the work-load. Soonimaya's story is a tribute to those who persist under these difficulties.

Every three years a soldier gets a furlough. He usually returns home, laden with gifts which have never been seen in the village. A few men do not go back into the army when their six-months leave is up, but many become professional soldiers, coming home for furloughs over a period of twenty years. On retirement, a man will have saved enough money to buy good land and build a fine house, and he will have a pension for the rest of his life.

The hill people have little grass for their cattle in wintertime; animals must feed on leaves gathered from the trees. Gathering fodder is a highly developed skill. Hill men become expert tree climbers. They cut the leaves, bundle them, and rope the bundles into big loads. It takes one man three or four hours to gather a load, and he can carry as much as 200 pounds at one time; but he will often need two of these loads to keep eight or nine cattle through the day.

A tailor is considered a very low-caste person. He has hereditary higher caste clients whom he must serve once or twice a year. If his work takes him more than a day, he is permitted to spend the night on the porch or in one of the cattle sheds, but he is not allowed into a Magar house.

The Perfect Husband

One way of being friendly in Nepal is to treat a person like a relative and to call him by a kinship term. The tiger may or may not be older than the fox but it is significant that the fox calls him "Elder Brother." By doing so he feels free to talk or joke with the tiger's wife, and he can even think of marrying her if the tiger dies. Such freedom with a *younger* brother's wife is not permitted.

How the Travelers Shared Their Meal

Every year when the farmers have finished planting their corn and millet a spring fair, or mela, is held in one of the larger trading towns. Villagers get up very early in the morning and travel many miles before sunrise, to the mela.

The hills of Nepal have few roads. Instead, foot trails stretch like a tangled web across the countryside. Spotted along these trails at frequent intervals are resting places, or chowtaras—large stone-terraced platforms, built around trees, about five feet above the ground. Here travelers can stop and rest in the shade or cook a meal above the dust of the trail. A chowtara is sometimes used as a school or as a meeting-place by the village headmen.

A chicken is eaten only on special occasions. Hill people subsist mainly on homemade beer and unsalted cornmeal mush. One can understand, then, why good food becomes an important topic of conversation, and a chicken frying in a pot brings out the worst in greedy men.

Bundar Bahadur Poon

The Nepalese hill people believe that the woods, fields, and waterfalls are inhabited by all kinds of evil spirits. These spirits, who are especially active at night, look and act like people. If they are not kept happy, they will strike out in many different directions—a child will fall ill and die, a buffalo will get blisters on his skin, crops will fail, or a father will fall from a tree. Offerings of special food are made at village and family shrines to appease these spirits so they will not be troublesome.

The Jackal and the Bear

In this story, as in other animal stories that do not include people, the main characters come together as "meets." This is a relationship which binds people together as "brothers" and gives each meet a new set of relatives. There are various ways of sealing this bond of friendship. They range from the simple exchange of a silver rupee to an elaborate ceremony performed by a Brahman, where gifts are exchanged and relatives are invited to witness and feast.

The Nepalese believe that the tragedies of life, such as sudden death or the loss of a crop overnight, have some connection with the stars. If the Brahman discovers a person's stars are in a very poor position, he suggests his client find a meet. This meet must be a person from another caste, whose stars are in a very strong position and who can deflect the trouble that lies ahead.

Another reason for finding a meet is a very practical one. Nepal is a country where hill people must walk to get from one place to another. In the fall, when Magar shepherds come down from the high pastures, back to their winter homes, they often make a ten-day trek to the trading town of Butwal, on the Indian-Nepalese border. Here they sell their summer produce of ghee for salt and cloth. This trip takes people out of their homeland and into country where they are strangers. If they have a meet in a village along the way, they are welcomed as one of the family and are given safe lodging for the night.

The Proud Father

The name of a child is very important. Children are named by the Brahman priest after they are born. A Nepalese hill child may have four names, one given to him for marriage and ceremonial occasions, one to remind the family of the season in which he was born, one to remind them of the day of the week on which he was born, and the last an everyday name which places him in the family as Jayta the eldest son, Myla the second, Syla the third, Kyla the fourth, etc.

Social graces are also very important. Ways of showing deference to superiors and complicated greeting patterns for relatives must be learned at an early age. If a man wishes to do business with another, he must first graciously accept refreshments and spend time discussing unrelated subjects.

Most boys and girls in hill Nepal are married by their parents between the ages of nine and sixteen. If marriages are postponed beyond these years, the young people may seek out their own mates, thus making it difficult for parents to arrange an alliance which they feel is more suitable.

The Stolen Jewel

This story shows the dependence of villagers on the local moneylender. Most hill people with small farms are able to grow only enough grain to cover their needs for that year. If a crop fails, or a plow-bullock dies, the farmer is forced to borrow. If the debt becomes too burdensome the farmer can send a child to work in the moneylender's home. More often he waits until a son is old enough to go into the army and can bring home money during his furlough.

Why the Flea Hops

In this story the quest for food becomes the central theme. Rice is considered the purest, most delicious grain to eat. Many poor farmers of Northern Nepal live too high to grow rice. For them, living as they do on seasonal diets of corn, wheat, barley, and potatoes, rice is a great luxury. Rice pudding is even more of a treat because the rice is cooked in milk. Shepherds with herds of buffaloes and cows produce a good deal of milk, but they keep little for themselves. Most of it is used to make ghee, which is carried to distant markets and sold for cloth, glass bangles, or spices—things hill people value which they cannot make themselves.

The King Who Rides a Tiger

When craft or professional people decide to marry only within their own group, they begin to form the kind of society found in the hills of Nepal. These groups develop rules of etiquette and behavior toward one another. Some do not eat with others; some do not smoke with others. Some groups, out of respect, may not even touch others. In the Hindu caste system of Nepal, the Brahman, traditionally a religious teacher, is considered to have the most prestige. Strangely enough, the toolmaker, the tailor, the fisherman, and the musician belong to groups with the least prestige. The Magar farmer lies somewhere in between.

Each caste feels it has certain virtues not shared by the other groups. Since *The King Who Rides a Tiger* is a story told by Magars about the three caste groups above them on the social ladder, we would expect to find some of the Magar attitudes towards these groups clearly expressed.

Magars are the traditional soldiers of Nepal; Brahmans are not. This has led to the universal Magar belief that Brahmans

are cowards and hypocrites, preaching one thing and practis-
ing another. In Magars' eyes, landlords are cruel and stingy,
and shopkeepers are more interested in money than in friendship. None of these attitudes are entirely justified. But know-
ing they exist makes reading the folk tale more meaningful.
We can understand what pleasure it must give Magar children
to hear that Mana Ras finally became king over all the people,
including the Brahman, the landlord, and the shopkeeper.

Lato, the Stupid One

A man who fishes for a living in Nepal, is considered a
landless outcaste. We can understand then, that when Myla, a
landowner and farmer, asks Lato why he does not fish for a
living, he is insulting him.

If someone could trace a folktale back to its beginnings, it
might not be recognized as the same tale at all. It has changed
with every story teller just as the word in the parlor game
changes when it is whispered from one child to the next. In
this story, we can tell where there was a change. In most hill
areas of Nepal, people call a shaman to their home when there
is illness. He will use possession by spirits to help him
determine the cause of a disease and its cure. Doctors who
treat illness in ways familiar to us, are not available. The only
contact these people had with the outside world was through
their young men who went to India to join the British army; so
we can be sure the part about the doctor in this story was
added by a former Gurkha soldier who had known about
western medicine.

The Soldier's Return

As seen in the story of Soonimaya, a career in the army is one
way hill Magars can pay off a debt. Some Nepalis go into the
army to seek adventure, or to find relief from the harsh hill
life. *The Soldier's Return* suggests that young men also go into
the army to escape difficulties they may have at home.

A shaman is asked to find the reason for many problems
such as a lost court case or a family quarrel. Sometimes the
cause of the problem is that someone in the family has become

a witch. If this is so, the shaman can help the troubled person by giving him a powerful protective charm to wear around his neck.

About the Animals in the Stories

In folk tales throughout the world, animals often perform feats of magic that people could never do. An example of this is seen in the story *Soonimaya* when the ants, the snakes, and the vulture help the girl solve her problems. But in many stories, like *The Jackal and the Bear,* the animals become "people" and do all the wise and foolish things people are capable of doing.

The folk tales in this book tell us something about the Nepalese attitude toward animals. The bear is considered slow-witted, the monkey very bright, and the jackal lazy and cunning even though he is not always successful with his tricks. And the animals play an important part in these stories because no one in the hill country could live without them. Buffaloes provide milk to make ghee, and sheep and goats provide wool to make blankets. Without ghee and wool a farmer would have nothing to trade for such necessities as salt, red peppers, and cloth for clothing. Animals also provide precious fertilizer for the crops. *The Stolen Jewel* clearly expresses the Nepalese feelings about the usefulness of animals.

However, animals are not always useful. Rats and monkeys eat tremendous amounts of grain. Jackals kill chickens. Insects, too, are annoying but important enough to find their way into a tale like *Why the Flea Hops.*

Animals in Nepalese folklore do not always behave in one story as they do in another. In *The Stolen Jewel* the rat is the ingenious organizer—the brains behind the efforts to get back the stolen jewel. In *The Proud Father* the rat seems to have great aspirations but little intelligence.

✾✾✾ Glossary

Ama	Mother
Ba	Father
baati	Small grass hut beside the trail; an overnight guest-house.
Bahadur	Brave; often used as a second name for boys.
bazaar	A cluster of small shops.
bhoot	An evil spirit.
boke-lagyo	Nepali for "I am hungry."
Brahman	Member of the highest caste; a priest and teacher.
Brahmani	The wife of a Brahman.
Bundar	A monkey.
choola	Small fireplace for cooking.
chowtara	A trail-side sitting platform built of stone; a resting place for travelers with heavy loads.
cummerbund	Long cloth wound around the waist.
dal	A pea, eaten with rice or ground corn.
dhoti	Cotton cloth about four yards long, worn by the hill men in place of trousers.
ghee	The liquid which remains after butter has been boiled and cooled.
Himalayas	The mountain range which divides Nepal from Tibet.
hooka	A large bubble-pipe in which the smoke is filtered through water before reaching the stem.
Jayta	Eldest son.
Jayti	Eldest daughter.
jungle	The Nepali word for "forest."
Koncha	Youngest son.

Konchi	Youngest daughter.
Krishna	One of the great Hindu gods, often pictured playing the flute. A name given to boys.
kukari	The famous Gurkha knife, used by most hill people for all their cutting needs.
Lato	Simpleton
lowry	Soldier
maana	A basic measure; one maana equals approximately one pint.
Magar	The tribe of people in Nepal from whom these stories were collected.
Magarni	Wife of a Magar.
meet	A friend from a different caste who is made an honorary member of the family.
Meetju	A respectful way of addressing one's meet.
mela	Fair, exhibition.
Mukiya	The headman of a village clan.
Myla	Second son.
Mylee	Second daughter.
Nepalese	Used as an adjective, meaning "of Nepal."
Nepali	Same as Nepalese.
peepul	A tree, considered by Hindus to be sacred because it is visited by the gods.
phutuk	A sound used by Magars to describe a frog's leap.
pice	1/100 of a rupee.
pondayra	Spring, or source of water flowing from the ground.
Poon	A Magar clan, often used as the third name: for example, Tek Bahadur Poon.
prate	An evil spirit.
Pundit-ji	Respectful form of address to a Brahman.
Rana	A Magar clan, not to be confused with a family of Chetris by the same name who once ruled Nepal.
rockshee	Distilled drink made of corn, rice, or millet.
rupee	A Nepalese coin worth about 14-1/2 cents in American money.

sahib	Influential person.
Sahib-ji	Form of address to an influential person.
sahu	Shopkeeper
sari	The cloth, five to six yards long, worn by women as a skirt or complete garment.
shaman	Curer, medicine man.
Syla	Third son.
Sylee	Third daughter.
taykee	A wooden pot made from a log, used to carry liquids.
topi	Cap
Tuck-a-brassi!	A Magar expression of jubilance, meaning "And what do you know!"
tumpline	A rope strap which is worn around the forehead to support a load carried on the back.
zamindar	Landlord
zamindarni	Landlord's wife.